A SERVANT
OF THE
GOVERNOR

For My Grandchildren
Tasha, Anna, Andrew and Thomas

A SERVANT OF THE GOVERNOR

Paul Duthie

y Lolfa

ISBN: 978 1 78461 1453

Published and printed in Wales
on paper from well-maintained forests by
Y Lolfa Cyf., Talybont, Ceredigion SY24 5HE
e-mail ylolfa@ylolfa.com
website www.ylolfa.com
tel 01970 832 304
fax 832 782

The history of the whole world contains not one single instance of oppression being put an end to by the humility of the oppressed.

William Cobbett

The power of the law consists of its terrors; if you wholly cease to hang, the common people will have nothing to fear: therefore you hang one now and then.

Edward Gibbon Wakefield,
Punishment of Death, 1831

I envy e'en the fly its gleams of joy
In the green woods; from being but a boy
Among the vulgar and the lowly bred,
I envied e'en the hare her grassy bed.

John Clare, 'Written in Prison'

1

J UST BEFORE DUSK Henry Cook reached down the double-barrelled gun from where it was hidden in the thatch, hanging it around his neck by a cord, so that it lay concealed beneath the copious folds of his dirty smock frock. The gun butt rested in a leather pouch at the bottom and where there were also large pockets in this conveniently enveloping garment. He shut the door of his cottage, freeing himself from its blunt odours of cold ash and fat. Cottage! It consisted of little more than four posts set in the ground to support cross beams, its cast-off windows were without frames or hinges and were merely stuck in the mud wall. Here and there the sun came in sharply through narrow gaps. The mouldering thatch was just higher than a man's head. Nearly twenty years ago, his father had simply squatted on the road verge of what was then the common and had speedily improvised the dwelling from hazel rods purloined from the adjacent woods, woven together and plastered with a daub of mixed clay, chalk, water, straw and cow dung. Since then the flimsy structure had solidified somewhat with wretched boards tacked together to serve for a table and a floor of broken pebble. Henry Cook, at nineteen, was a man of independent means – and spirit. A master poacher could stay off the parish books. But in terms of the social order he was the lowest of the low, a squatter, and the son of a squatter.

The shotgun was the treasured prize of a fracas between his father and a keeper, and as he adjusted it slightly for comfort, his eye was drawn to the dying yellow flowers of the leeks. Grown in the thatch as a charm against lightning, they held the last of the day's light. He pulled his black greasy hat down low and tight over his black greasy hair which tended to curl. Since the enclosures the roads had become the danger on Cook's journey. Only ten years ago he would have been able to travel the whole distance to Barrents' plantation across commons and heath lands, save for a dash over the still unfenced turnpike. But like his father, that world was gone.

The sky began to stain with the mauve haze of sunset. It was nearly dark. His cracked, nailed boots trod on dead leaves the colour of tobacco in the familiar lane. His glance was not arrested by the familiar row of his near neighbours' rain-worn, airless cottages. The windows broken and the holes stuffed with rags, or covered with rotten pieces of board; the walls crumbling, the thatch rotten, the chimneys leaning, the doors but bits of doors. The reek of the ditch behind them, which acted as both cesspool and sewer, and which allowed the contents of pigsties, privies and rubbish pits to flow into the open gutter of the lane whenever it rained, also seemed to go unnoticed. As did the silence, the silence of hunger, pain, sickness. He looked to the sky, scuffed with faint, thin swirls of high cloud. And to the overarching trees – old trees, almost leafless now – walnut, yew, larch, and saw two crows lift in the rising wind. A good omen. It promised to be a star-lit night, moon enough to outline roosting pheasants against the sky, and with enough wind to cover the sound of snapped twigs underfoot. By morning frost would be fingering the grass. Once settled the birds would be reluctant to stir from the tree branches. With luck a single, well aimed blast might bring down half a dozen.

Almost, it would seem, from the time Henry Cook had crawled from the earth floor of his parents' hovel out into the vastness of woods and commons surrounding the little village of Micheldever, he was so close to the natural world that he himself might almost be considered a part of it. It was a sea of green – a world of springy grass tussocks, flaming gorse, purple moor grass, great patches of thistles and dark holly. A place of mysterious woods canopied by ancient trees, of fleshy toadstools, pennywort and shade plants – foxgloves, mints, sweet woodruff. In summer kingfishers and darting swallows haunted the streams and there were forests of swaying grasses six feet high, in which a small boy might disappear and idly listen to the chink of tiny russet-brown wrens. How old was he when he had stumbled upon a partridge nest with its pale olive eggs on its cushion of dry grass and leaves? When did he first see the plump brown birds in early morning when their wings were heavy with dew? Why, a wandering boy might all but step on a partridge and could scarcely be expected to know it was reserved for gentlemen only.

As a boy of twelve years old he had helped his father set snares. He had looked down on the leverets in their form built in the long grass, creatures born open-eyed, fully furred and active. He was unlettered and superstitious, but he knew the brown hare was a creature of habit. Through the day it would rest, its long ears alert, a large lustrous eye with the honey-coloured iris always open. At nightfall, it would move off on its long foraging journeys. And at each dawn it would return by the same track, to pass through the same meuse, or gate, beneath the hedge. A hare caught in a snare screams a shock child-like shriek, which could bring the keepers from half a mile away. Not so Henry Cook's snares. Set eight inches high, with a twig bent over it to make the hare lower its head, his snares were loose-pegged, yet secure. They were set with hands washed in the stream, then rubbed in the surrounding soil.

He crossed the stubbled remains of a hard-worked barley field, moved quietly through clumps of nettles at its edge and halted in the dark shade of the wood. He stood and listened. Nothing. At last he was able to take the gun from beneath his clothing. At the next step he was momentarily startled by wood-pigeons, their wings crashing among branches and twigs above him. Nothing to fear there! Regaining his composure, he heard the crack-voiced cock-pheasants' 'cu-uck, cuck' and the wheezy whistle of the hens. The game birds were rising to their roosts. He would wait a little longer – steady himself. He caught the quick flicker of a fox disappear in the late autumn bronze.

There was no need to look out for the trip-wires of spring guns or for man-traps. Even if they were not now banned by law, Sir Thomas Barrents was too sensible a man to employ such means of indiscriminate destruction. Nor had they posed a great threat in his father's time, as their locations were well known thanks to communication between villagers and estate workers. More humane owners employed a toothless variety which merely crushed but did not tear; some had teeth two inches long. When opened, the trap formed a complete circle between two and three feet in diameter. It took the whole weight of the person who set it or 'toiled it' to force the spring into place. He did not know that the Duke of Wellington voted for the return of the man-trap with the same steadfastness with which he supported the lash in the ranks of the army. He did know that if he were caught by a keeper it would mean seven years transportation.

He moved stealthily towards the place he had heard the pheasants roosting. In the fitful moonlight it was not hard to see the dark shapes of the birds, motionless, blobs against the sky. Cook slowly raised the gun to his shoulder, steadied his breathing. He was not conscious of his final caress of the trigger, nor of the heavy recoil from the old gun. A thick cloud of black smoke unrolled in front of him as if that were creating the frightful noise which lengthened, hollowed out and died in the darkness leaving the air vibrating. He took to his heels. He had no dog. His heart racing he searched the long grass.

Yes! One. Two. No, three! All cleanly killed. He would not be taken. He was not a tall man but he was at the height of his physical powers. He would loose a charge of shot at the feet of a keeper if he had to. But there was no pursuit. He was free to return under the cover of the night through the deep runnels of half-abandoned tracks and secret pathways to safety with the satisfying weight of the birds thumping against his legs.

A single pheasant could bring four to five shillings. He had endured endless labour of bent-backed slavery in the fields for as little as seven shillings a week during the summer. And he had no prospect of much winter work thanks to the advent of the threshing machines and mole-ploughs the farmers were so keen on. Had he not heard the overseer boast that one machine could complete in a few days the work which had kept men busy with the flail for weeks in warm barns? A dry rot of resentment welled up within him as he remembered the sight of paupers, men degraded to the level of beasts of burden, yoked like cattle in the shafts of a cart or a wheelbarrow, to draw rocks to the highway for a grudging handout from the parish. This while the holy reverend enjoyed his comfortable tithe, slept on a feather bed and drank his wine. It rankled like a stone in his shoe. Thank God for men like Joseph Mason. The thought of the man cheered him and he remained only a few moments in the lonely cold of his cottage before renewing his tramp, this time through the inky darkness towards Bullington. No longer burdened with the weight and awkwardness of the gun, and buoyed a little with the evening's success, he walked quickly singing quietly to himself: 'A shiny night is my delight in this season of the year.'

The cottage was recessed from the road and laurel bushes grew to the height of the windows. On either side of the mossy path were the remnants of a large summer garden with a few coarse cabbages still struggling to hold onto life. He knocked on the blue door and waited for some moments before it was opened about six inches revealing a woman's anxious face.

'Henry! Come in. Do,' she said in a relieved voice, pushing her fair hair back from her forehead with her wrists and making way for him.

'I'm sorry, Ann. Are Joseph and Robert not at home?'

'Yes, but they have been as restless as a flock of starlings since they have heard the news from Kent.'

'From Kent?' asked Cook, uncomprehendingly.

Rising from his chair at a scrubbed deal table, Joseph Mason removed his reading glasses revealing a face which was a mixture of coarseness and sensitivity and smiled warmly at the youth. 'Yes, much news indeed from the men in Kent,' he said as he dropped the glasses on a now folded copy of Cobbett's *Register*. 'Much news indeed.'

Younger than Joseph by some six years, his brother Robert appeared in the doorway of a small room leading off from the main interior of the cottage. He was dressed in a collarless flannel shirt and his feet were bare as if he were ready for bed, but his eyes brightened as he nodded a welcome to Henry.

'You will tell us all at the Swan on Wednesday?' asked Henry, his coffee-coloured eyes full of interest.

'Yes, at Sutton, our esteemed Sir Thomas has this place in too firm a grip,' replied Robert in a quiet, but constrained manner.

Ann beckoned to Henry to take a seat. But he shook his head. She was a small woman, lithe and wiry, she may have been thirty, still pretty, or would have been but for the crumpled tiredness of her nerve-worn face. He had interrupted her washing potatoes in a chipped enamel dish. Her hands were red and rough.

'It's late and I'll stay but a moment,' he said, lowering his voice as he saw the sleeping bundle of warmth and blond curls of a child in a small bed, and, near the square open fire of turf and snap wood, old Mrs Mason in the inglenook. Her hair was as white as frost, her dark eyes too piercing to be genial. 'I have summat for ye. Change from the taters and shake.'

The pheasant which he produced from the folds of his garment and placed on the bare wood of the table beside the dish of dirtied water seemed to emit a pale sheen in the shadowy spaces of the room. Its dead eyes glittered yellow in the hanging purple head, the carmine and golden hues glowed like iridescent dyes. Comfort and riches for a week!

The old lady half rose and with an excited tremor edging her voice proclaimed, 'He'll go three pounds, that one, he will.'

'Oh, but Henry!' exclaimed Ann, her sea-grey eyes widening with vague anxiety.

'Now Ann,' said Joseph, giving her a light reassuring kiss on the top of her head, 'did not the Lord create the beasts of the field and the birds of the air for all – not just for gentlemen?'

'If there be fault,' said Henry, deeply satisfied, 'it be the faults of our betters.' He began his way to the door. 'Wednesday then,' he nodded to Robert.

'Thank you, Henry,' Joseph said simply as he opened the door to the now cold night air, 'but be careful. Very careful.'

He watched Henry walk into the darkness. The wind had dropped and there was a powdering of frost on the ground. He felt a quick shiver and closed the door against the cold.

Ann was drying her hands on a white cloth. The sleeping child suddenly gave out a thin, tight wail, rolled over on the little bed and resumed her slumbers.

'That boy looks to you so much,' Ann said quietly looking at the child.

'I know. I hope he won't be disappointed. He has had a hard time of it since his father died.'

THE JOURNAL OF LADY BARRENTS 1830

*T*HE MONTHS OF *January and February were months of severe cold – much suffering attended the state of the poor as the preceding summer was too wet to enable them to get in the turf that these people use for fuel. The cold continued until the end of March. On the first of April there was a considerable fall of snow but the remainder of the month proved extraordinarily warm and bright. It would seem that the illness of King George began with that fall of snow. However, as the secrecy about everything that was going on at Windsor Castle was quite impenetrable, expectations that the King would be able to have a drawing room on St George's Day were kept up until a few days before the 23rd.*

Everybody in London is afraid of naming distant days for their balls and parties, lest the expected death of the King should put a stop to all gaiety. Discontented murmurs began to grow loud from dressmakers and milliners who put off their journeys in search of spring fashions fearing to embark in large purchases when perhaps only black bombazine would be called for. Indeed it became almost a fashion in London to go to fine places in old dresses on the pretence of the expected mourning, instead of it being held a heinous offence against the laws of dress to wear the same habiliments two evenings following.

Madame Lalande was the new woman at the opera this season. She is considered to be a most accomplished singer, but I found her voice thin and reedy. Lablache, the man, has a most magnificent and powerful one. As for Mademoiselle Taglioni, if dancing and standing en pointe *can be called a science, she excelled, but fashion is certainly not her charm. Oh, that drop pearl headdress and tiered skirt! On the English stage, much debased and little thought of in these modern times, Miss Fanny Kemble, a niece and protégée of Mrs Siddons, possessed some attraction. She is a young and unfinished actress but has the advantage of a pretty person.*

The middle of May and the King's doubtful state continues. We dine with the Duke of Norfolk tonight; at Almack's, Wednesday; Landsdowne House, Friday; a party here, Saturday.

A Bill for putting the Jews on the same footing with dissenting Christians was brought forward and mercifully defeated in the House of Commons. My own feelings, I confess, revolt at the idea of a Jew and a Christian being equal, even in this liberal age. I could never reconcile such an idea to myself.

George IV lingered on until the 26th of June. The Duke and Duchess of Clarence were in bed when the Duke of Wellington came to announce the Duke's accession to the throne. The new King, finding it was yet early, returned to bed, saying that he wished particularly to do so, having never been in bed with a queen before! William IV's very easy manners and the amiable qualities of Queen Adelaide have endeared them to us all. Although the King walking alone about the streets, as he did at first, was considered infra dig, *I think it much in accord with the temper of the times.*

In the autumn the King and Queen went to Brighton, where they were received with grateful enthusiasm. A triumphal arch was erected near the entrance of the town with sailors and children waving colours. The effect was said by people of good judgement to be very beautiful. The populace met the King and Queen on the road and wished to draw the carriage; but the King would not allow the horses to be taken off. He called to the people, 'You want to see me, and I want to see you, so you may depend on my going a foot's pace, but I request you to let the horses draw us.'

In this manner they proceeded. They remain at the Pavilion, where, mirabile dictum, *they have large family parties and other company daily at dinner, which are spoken of as realising the ideas of the entertainment described in the* Arabian Nights.

2

THE WOMAN, SCARVED and tired-eyed, was bent over a heavy wooden tub set on a flat quern stone washing metal plates and mugs outside her cottage in a wind that threw chill chips of rain. The grey, greasy water exposed her chapped hands. Her knuckles were inflamed and swollen. She straightened.

'How's Mrs Deacle keepin'?' she asked with dulled interest into the wind.

'She is fair to middling, but is not looking forward to the winter,' he replied.

She said nothing else but was happy enough for him to leave his horse, a heavy legged, sway-backed plodder, in her overgrown orchard for an hour or so. There it could find a wizened apple or two amongst the dying weeds and thistles while he was in town. Her eyes gleamed bright as gin when he placed a few pennies beside her on the flat stone she used as a washstand. She smiled her acknowledgement, plunged her hands into the tub and began to hum quietly to herself.

Deacle, a small tenant farmer on a poor holding, trudged in heavy boots towards Sutton Scotney the largest of the villages along the road beside the tiny River Dever. With Wonston, Stoke Charity and Micheldever to the east and Bullington, Barton Stacey and Chilbolton to the west, Sutton was the natural centre of the valley. It also straddled the London road and heard news of all sorts as carriers brought gossip, newspapers, ideas and letters into the area. But today there were few people about. There was little for sale and little to spend. He had come to collect a length of chain from the blacksmith – and to hear what was happening in Kent from Enos Diddams. Diddams, master shoemaker and reputed linkman with William Cobbett himself, was the leader of the local Radical and Musical Society which met regularly at the White Swan, an old style beer house of mellow red brick, ivy and ancient dark beams. There, local tradesmen including harness makers, sawyers, butchers and shopkeepers as well as farm labourers, free for a while from the watchful eye of their masters, could discuss their lot and what could be done about it. But whether comfortably ensconced in the White Swan or at his place of work, Diddams always knew what lay at the heart and source of any rumour muttering its course through village or field. And the talk at the moment was all of Kent.

Deacle reached the small town square. A girl, a thin and gangling child, perhaps she was twelve, held a ragged and shrill sibling by the hand as she stretched up to her full height to look longingly at some loaves and glazed buns behind the misted glass of a small shop. The little domestic scene had the force of intimate truth for Deacle. Too many have been reduced to peering and peeping helplessly at the riches and plenty of others, he thought with some bitterness. Farm labourers ate unwashed cold potatoes in clear view of barns full of corn that they themselves had produced. Men near starving on parish relief mended roads while sheep grazed on the other side of the hedge. The open fields were alive with hares but poor families had not tasted meat for months. He stepped around scythes, bill-hooks and other farm implements which littered the pavement outside the ironmonger's. The wind now blew with such malice that he pulled the collar of his coat more firmly about him. He was looking forward to the leaping heat of the forge. He could hear the cling, cling of the blacksmith's hammer. But first he would call on Enos.

Enos Diddams sat in a full-length apron on a three-legged stool holding a boot in a wooden vice between his knees. He looked up and smiled when Deacle entered his little workshop. His forehead was wrinkled deeply emphasising eyes brimming with a concentrated intelligence behind glittering spectacles. The clutter about him was amazing. Three hammers of various sizes and makes lay at his feet. Leather, rolled or cut into different shapes and patterns, lay in apparent disarray on a dusty wooden bench amongst large-eyed needles, coarse twine, blades and awls of different sizes. Racks of shoes and boots in varying states of disrepair lined an entire wall. A poster, faded and yellowing, advertised an extract of soap. A once-coloured landscape had faded to sepia brown. But his greeting was as warm as the little shop itself which commanded an uninterrupted view of the square. Moving a heavy last he cleared a space for the farmer.

'And how be ye and yer good wife?' he asked cordially.

The image of the girl at the shop window returned to Deacle as he settled his considerable bulk on an ancient chair.

'Yes. We are quite well, I suppose', he said rather solemnly, 'but one needs the patience of Job in times like these.'

'They're not showing much of that in Kent at present,' Enos remarked, while removing a tack he held between his lips. There was excitement in his voice. He directed his glance to three or four newspapers near his feet. 'Flour carts overturned, wheat sacks slit, windows broken, hayricks burned, machinery mangled!' He turned on his stool, bullied open a stubborn drawer, took out a handled blade and began to lightly trim the sole of the boot he held. 'On Monday last there was a parish meeting held at Benenden. The overseer was sitting at the pay table. Someone shot at him through the closed window! Fortunately for him, he had at that precise instant leant forward to speak privately to a person beside him.' Enos stooped, picked up a paper and searched for the article. He read: '"Upon examination, the curtain which hung before the window had marks of twenty-seven shots which had perforated it. Immediately a search was made, but the night being very dark, the guilty person was not discovered." Kent is on fire! If the flames reach Sussex the government will panic!'

'It's a wonder the peace has been kept as long as it has, if you ask me. Overseer, you say,' said Deacle meditatively into the short silence which had developed. 'Assistant overseer more than likely, a hireling from distant parts and paid a salary no doubt. That man will not be your old-fashioned overseer, mark my words. The work of grinding down starving men is too painful for the delicate nerves of the rich. He would be a recruit from outside the parish. That's my guess. Such men are not liked.'

'There are many who are not liked,' said Diddams evenly. He paused at his work and looked directly at the farmer. 'You will be with us at the Swan on Wednesday night? We must be ready.'

'Aye, to be sure, I'll be there.'

There was a clatter and clip of hooves on stones and the clink of harness in the street. The London coach drew to a halt outside the White Swan on the opposite side of the square. The blinkered horses steamed and stamped in the cold wet air. Two passengers, a man and a woman, alighted and picked their way carefully over treacherous cobbles to the inn. Enos and Deacle saw Henry Cook approach the coach driver. They stood shoulder to shoulder, bulky smock frock to wide oilskin, forming a curtain which shrouded the side of the coach. The driver scratched the back of his neck. Then they parted. Cook moved away quickly pulling his hat down tightly over his eyes. The coachman rummaged for a moment under his seat then turned to the Swan where the man and woman sat in front of the roasting kitchen fire and busied themselves with hot porter and a helping of boiled brisket.

Enos Diddams chuckled and gave Deacle a shrewd sidelong

look. 'I suspect there may be one or two dead passengers on the way to an innkeeper somewhere between here and London this evening. Someone who prides himself on his table and the quality of the game he can provide.'

'He's a decent lad, Cook,' said Deacle quietly. 'He deserves better than digging field ditches and lifting swedes twelve hours a day for a pittance.'

'Perhaps a better life awaits him if the mobs in Kent hold sway.'

Henry Cook slowed his pace; his hand nuzzled into his pocket and he gently felt the newly won coins between thumb and fingers. A faint satisfied smile played about his lips.

'Hey, you there!'

The words struck him like a hook and pulled him violently round to face the man. It was Barrents' steward, Francis Callendar. He sat on a large black gelding. He had the face of a martinet. A recalcitrant mouth and jaw set rigid. His hair was rust-red, limp, over eyes of a vibrant greyness. How long had he been there? He suppressed the rising urge to look back at the coach. Both the sale and purchase of game were unlawful. His mind clouded with an unpleasant muzziness. He tried to settle his breathing. Callendar watched him steadily with a look as sharp as glass.

'In town on business I suppose,' said Callendar with withering sarcasm and a cold laugh at the thought of the likes of Henry Cook transacting business.

Afraid the man would catch something in the tone of his voice, Cook said nothing. The steward leaned forward placing more of his weight on the stirrups. The saddle creaked. Cook smelt the resinous leathery smell of it. The black horse gave a slight shake to its head as the bit loosened.

'We've had some trouble in the woods of late.' His voice was flat and lingered in a short, tense silence. 'A man with a gun the keeper tells me.'

Cook met his gaze. They struggled in a net of mutual resentment. 'You have made an arrest then?' he asked in a carefully contrived neutral voice.

A quick wave of irritation crossed the steward's face. The corner of his lip curled in sour anger.

'Not yet. No. But the keeper tells me there won't be much to arrest if he and his watchers catch up with the low dog.'

He wheeled his horse, spat wetly onto the road and galloped off so abruptly that the horse's hooves flung mud into the air.

Cook stood for a moment or two in the damp heavy smells of the street, the wind bullied and tugged at his clothes. He felt the quick bite of hatred. Impotent rage was the worst of its kind, he knew, but it surged through his blood. 'What would you have me be,' he muttered bitterly, 'pauper or poacher?'

He moved on oblivious to his surroundings until he was outside the smithy. The blacksmith worked in front of the red-black maw of the forge. Seeing Cook, he raised a powerful arm holding a heavy hammer in recognition. Somehow the action gladdened him, but in spite of the chill air he did not join him. He was anxious to leave the town for some reason obscurely felt for the freedom of trees and wind. Shafts of pale light fell out of a sky brimmed with cloud. Only the silver willows and dark green elms held their summer colour. Swallows flickered above his head. He slowly regained his composure. Once more he came to terms with the given circumstances of his life. He even smiled a little wryly. Thanks to Callendar's threats the gun would be at home for the next few nights. He would work the wind-wild country of open fields with net and snare and try his luck for hares and partridge.

3

A s THEY WENT into the White Swan, the gritty stone-flag floor of which was a step below the passage, which in turn was a step below the road outside, Joseph and Robert Mason were instantly greeted by several members of the Radical and Musical Society who were seated on backless benches at a long lumpish table. The brothers registered the pleasant, close fug of the room, the lambent glint of brass and pewter above a glowing fire, the few stools pushed awkwardly against a barrel under the cobwebbed window. Before each man was a hooped mug of brown ale. Unlike Bullington which was kept under the close scrutiny of Sir Thomas Barrents and his nephew Mr Bingham Barrents whose mansion in the Palladian vogue lay no further than a mile from his uncle's Doric-columned portico, Sutton was still considered an open village where conversation did not need to be sibilant and guarded.

'Some ale for the Masons there,' said Deacle, with forced good cheer. He was well respected by his workers for being a fair man. Unlike most of his station he considered it absolutely necessary for the management of his farm to work as hard as his labourers.

'Not tea?' asked the Sutton blacksmith with bitter superciliousness, his forge-red face pouched and heavy. His sixty-year old frame was still powerful despite his thinning iron-grey hair. In his youth he had once been the toast of the valley when he would not concede defeat in the once popular game of single-stick. His head was swollen, one eye was closed up, and both arms and both sides were badly bruised. But he continued to face his combatant who had not drawn the regulation one inch of blood from his skull and won the thirty guineas of prize money – more than the annual wage of a Hampshire labourer. It was not until later when he was dividing the prize money among all the contestants that he had gleefully revealed that he had swallowed a broken tooth out of fear that if he spat out the enamel the free blood would run the fateful inch.

'They're men! Give them bread, bacon and beer and to hell with yer tea and taters!'

This came loudly and sullenly from a labourer from East Stratton. His life mildewed by rasping want, his beard was long and ragged, his forehead sallow. He had struck the table violently. His scabby hands remained there, the fingers bent from the continual embrace with the eye of the spade.

The unanchored talk around the table instantly dissolved in the intimate melancholy and acid anger of the man. Joseph Mason caught the movement of Henry Cook as he briefly placed his arm on the labourer's thin hunched shoulders to comfort him. Joseph recalled his father saying that in his day every man in the village brewed his own beer. Now, not a single man in the parish did so. Taxes on malt and hops had doubled since that time. A labourer no longer carried a wooden bottle of beer slung over his shoulder to the fields but a few cold potatoes in his satchel and tea or at least some warm water which passed for tea. It was not uncommon to see men dry as cattle quenching their thirst in turn from the water pump.

The sudden, oppressive silence was broken by the gravelly tones of the blacksmith who sang robustly if not altogether tunefully in order to make his contempt for the weaker beverage clear:

Tea kettle and potato plot
What black-arsed things they be,
Wealth has made these the workman's lot,
Can such a land be free?

Joseph Mason appeared not to have heard the blacksmith; he felt an almost suffocating swelling of pity intensify into anger. He studied the Stratton man. Like so many others who raised bread for others to eat, he was trapped in a squalid, sickening weariness of work and routine. Poverty gnawed at his nerves. He looked ill, exhausted. His face glistened in the fire light from an unhealthy sheen of sweat. He was as helpless as a rat in a bucket.

Enos Diddams rose from his seat at the head of the table. He did not have the ruddy wind-burned complexion of men who spent their time out of doors. His alert, intelligent eyes and grey hair which shone white in the light gave him a bookish, scholarly look. He lifted and dropped the latest *Register* upon the table with his left hand, rapped the table with an ancient pewter spoon with his right and spoke in a clear, assertive voice.

'Thank ye, blacksmith. Thank ye.' His eyes also targeted the Stratton man. 'Now let's have a chorus or two of "Roast Beef of Old England" – you know the words and Robert can give us the lead. It puts some heart back into a man.'

No further prompt was needed. The room thrilled to deep, varied voices:

In Queen Bess's days, and at much later date,
How happy indeed was an Englishman's state,
For although he toiled both early and late;
'Twas for the roast beef of Old England.

Of saucepans and candlesticks too he'd a stock,
And what he most valu'd, a good eight-day clock,
In cellar a barrel of beer upon cock,
To drink with the roast beef of Old England.

Now, instead of roast beef, a red herring you see,
And a most wretched hovel, entirely free
Of every comfort that used to be
The boast and the pride of Old England.

Alas! What a change, and how alter'd the case!
The toiling remains, but all else has given place
To that which to mention bespeaks the disgrace
Of those who have ruled Old England.

Enos remained standing, 'Now before ye quench yer thirst, I raise a jug to the men of Kent. Kent has risen my sonnies, ricks have been burned, machines broken and overseers ridded by way of the parish dung cart. Wages have been agreed on. Their leaders have paid the price of a caution and three days in prison.' Here, he paused, adjusted his glasses and read from the *Register*: '"It is no new feeling of discontent at work," says Cobbett, "it is a long harboured resentment, and it has now bursted forward."' He continued in a quieter, more controlled voice, '"They have always been told that their acts of violence, and particularly the burnings, can do them no good, but add to their wants, by destroying the food that they would have to eat. But they know better: they know that one threshing-machine takes wages from ten men; and they know that *they* will have none of this food – potatoes and salt do not burn! It is unquestionable that their acts have produced good and great good too. The poor have only themselves to blame when starvation stalks the land, if they lie down like dogs and die with hunger."' He paused emphasising the import of the words, and then resumed his seat without further comment.

'Aye, there's a sight I'd enjoy,' said the Stratton man. 'Barrents' man between the shafts of the cart. The egg-sucking cur!'

'Who? Callendar?' asked Cook.

'Aye, that be he in his fine black boots and perched up on his fine black horse. I would like to prise the eye out of the head of that gelding with a chisel one dark night!'

Joseph Mason shook his head violently as if to free himself of the idea and was about to speak, but Joseph Carter, the club's treasurer, had already begun.

'Ecod man, we don't want to do any mischief of that kind here. We want our children to go to bed with a full belly instead of crying. We want twelve shillings a week and the chance to earn it.' He paused, gave a grave smile. His face had reddened emphasising a map of broken veins in his cheeks. It was a long speech for the usually silent man and he hadn't finished. 'What with parsons and piano-fortés, farmers fat as jugs, with carpets and parlour-bells and hardly a smock frock to be seen for top boots and fine skin gloves, the good old ways have gone to the dogs right enough – upon my carcass they have. But what would I do with a parlour-bell? I be's Joseph Carter, thatcher and hedger. I never had a book put afore me never in my life, not as I minds on, but I still knows what I want. I want enough to cut and carve for meself. I want cheese and bread – not cold potatoes. I want a bottle of beer and not lie on me belly at a stream.'

'Aye, it's the fellows in nail-shoes do the work,' said the younger Mason with a steely majesty.

A gnarled old man nodded sagely. He removed a clay pipe from between smoke-blackened teeth before speaking. 'Masters never give us a chance to speak to them,' he said querulously. The years had traced deep lines on his mottled red face. 'I can mind a time when we was paid at the fire-side over a mug of ale. Now it be poked at ye through a window of some outhouse by the steward or his man.'

The Stratton man raised his turbid, bloodshot eyes and

spoke again. His hair was matted and wild; his gums were white.

'Damn them! Fire the ricks. I work twelve hours a day to give them food, if they give me none of it, they shall have none of it at any rate.' His face became blotched with exertion. He had none of Joseph Carter's gentle strength. 'We can't be worse off. If we are took we shall have summat to eat.'

'I know how 'tis done,' said Henry Cook, 'the ricks. The risk is small.'

'Sparks from the fires in Kent will fly as far north as Carlisle before this winter is out,' said Enos. 'In their fear owners will break their own machines before we can lay a hammer to them. But there is something we can do tonight – now. I propose a petition to the King.'

'The King?' said the blacksmith and Deacle together in baffled amazement.

'Yes, the King. Every man has the right to petition his sovereign for a redress of grievances. Cobbett has done it and we shall do it. And as Joseph is the best scholar amongst us I ask him to write it.'

The restless, shadowy figure of the Stratton man was silent. The movement around the table was stilled. All were alert interest – a little overwhelmed by the magnitude of the suggestion.

Enos continued composedly enough, although his eyes were as bright as some woodland predator.

'Are we in agreement that we acquaint the King of our wants?'

'Aye!'

Here Enos paused and looked steadily into the dark gloomy eyes of Henry Cook.

'Are we also in agreement that no man will take action until we learn the conclusion of it?'

'Aye.'

Enos could not be certain if Cook had contributed to the resonant rumble of assent or not.

'And my wife and I will take great pleasure in visiting the villages hereabouts to collect signatures for ye,' said Deacle. 'We have been screwed down too long, I say – too long!'

'And perhaps two or three pence apiece from those who can?' suggested Carter quietly, 'to help Joseph on his way.'

'Agreed,' said Enos with alacrity. 'Let's stand then and raise a toast to William Cobbett, friend of the poor and a true man of England!'

In the blue-grey darkness outside the Swan, Joseph Mason's breath misted in the cold motionless air. Robert would tell him if anything else of importance was discussed. He could remain no longer indoors. He soon passed the thin scattering of darkened houses and as he walked beside the shirred waters of a rushing stream he breathed in the resinous night scents around him. An owl hooted. Their sound would become more common as winter came on. He was deeply excited. He would write to the King! It was something that he could do; something that he must do well. Had not his mother reminded him often enough when she had kept a dame school that Ben Jonson had once been a bricklayer and Robbie Burns a ploughman like himself? That it was workmen who built the great cathedral of Salisbury? His mind raced ahead already at work on what he would say. *Kings and governments were instituted to protect the weak against the strong, the poor against the unjust encroachments of the rich, in short, to watch over and protect the welfare and happiness of the people.* No! No! There must first be an acknowledgement of the King as lawful sovereign. He stopped, then began to pace up and down in the valuable silence of a high-walled lane oblivious to the cold frost-filled air. *We complain that many of us have not food sufficient to satisfy our hunger; our drink is chiefly the crystal element; we have not clothes to hide the nakedness of ourselves, our wives, and our children, nor fuel wherewith to warm us.* It would take days of concentrated effort.

'You're so late, Joseph, I was beginning to worry. And Robert still not home? Is everything alright?' asked Ann, when he made his way quietly into his cottage.

She was in bed but had not been asleep. The fire, a mere glow, offered little light and less warmth.

'It must be nearly midnight. What's wrong Joseph?'

'Nothing's wrong. There is no need to worry.' He spoke in little more than a whisper as he looked at his sleeping child warmly wrapped in her cradle. 'I am to go to Brighton with a petition to the King. I am to write it!' he added breathlessly. 'Some good may come of it, Ann.' He took off his boots and started at his heavy outer garments.

'Brighton! But Brighton must be sixty miles away. How will you get there? And at this time of the year, Joseph!' Her voice was full of concern.

'Hey! You are talking to a man who could run a mile in under five minutes in his day. A man whose previous employer, one Mr Fitzwater of Cranbourne, would make bets with his friends on whether I could leap a gate or hedge knowing full well I could clear it as easily as a kangaroo!' said Joseph smiling faintly as he snuggled deep into the warm bedding. 'I will walk to Brighton, Ann. All will be well. Go to sleep.'

He moulded his body to her shape with his knees behind hers and felt the warmth and weight of her on his upper legs and thighs. He put his arm around her. And waited. Soon he heard the steady breathing of his sleeping wife. The silence kneaded into his ears; he thought of the cold outside, the frost numbing the countryside – miles and miles of it. But he could not sleep. His mind would not rest. Words, fragments of sentences, ideas, swirled and competed with each other. *We complain that not one of Your Majesty's petitioners has ever been allowed to vote at an election; that right being confined to the rich, men in whom the people have no confidence. We complain that tithes are paid to rich men in the church.* He rolled over onto his other side, careful not to disturb Ann. The bare sole of his foot found hers; he curled his toes over hers tenderly. *We complain of excessive taxes on the necessaries of the poor man's life: malt, hops, soap, candles. We complain, that notwithstanding the misery and half starvation to which we are reduced, the law forbids us to take for our own use the wild birds and animals that inhabit the woods and fields; those being kept for the sports of the rich.* His last conscious thought was of Henry Cook.

THE JOURNAL OF LADY BARRENTS 1830

*T*HE MONTH OF *August was distinguished by the tragic folly of the King of France, Charles X. The whole royal family were obstinate in their belief that they were in no danger until street lamps were shattered, shops looted and barricades erected in the streets of Paris by angry mobs. Such a disturbance will probably excite a revolutionary spirit not only in France but throughout Europe. Foreigners and the lower classes can always be relied upon to cause trouble! At Cherbourg the Dauphiness and the Duchess de Berri were robbed of their clothes, and on their arrival at Cowes were obliged to be supplied by Lady Anglesey and Lady Grantham for immediate use. Lady Grantham invited the French royal party to luncheon, and Lady Listowel to tea the day of the regatta, but this was declined. Mr Humphrey Ward offered Lulworth Castle as a temporary asylum and there they remain having journeyed from Rambouillet by packet steamer.*

According to Lady Frampton of Moreton House, the French royals with the exception of the King himself, and much to the amusement of all ranks, are wont to visit neighbouring families, often on foot. They are so unlike English people! Lady Frampton herself was surprised by the Duchesse d'Angoulême and an attendant lady called Madame de St Maur quite early one morning while she was busy letter writing. Their dress was inferior to that of most housekeepers: the Duchess in a shabby yellowish shawl, cotton stockings and very short petticoats. And both wore coarse, weather-beaten straw bonnets! Their equipage was a miserable low four-wheeled open carriage with two seats drawn by a rough pony. No servant was with them. Their only travelling companion was an old handsome dog that walked about perfectly at his ease, as if accustomed to such visits. They stayed half an hour and left in a heavy shower.

The King does not leave the castle. He is a fine, tall, gentlemanly man and the good done to the poor since his arrival is said to be great. He permits nothing to appear a second time on the royal table, and so it is given to the poor.

4

THE REVEREND JAMES Joliffe, curate of Barton Stacey and nearly forty, woke with the impression that he had experienced a sharp pain in the stomach while sleeping and hoped that it would not recur. He rolled onto his back cushioning his head against the soft pillow. He could not be ill this morning. Not today when he had planned his sermon so carefully. He was buoyed a little by the thought of standing above his congregation in the high pulpit; looking down on their upturned faces intently listening to him. But his insides did feel suspiciously restless. Where was the woman? Didn't she know it was Sunday? Did she want to interrupt him on his chamber pot! Thankfully, he heard measured footsteps in the hallway followed by a light knocking on his door.

'Yes,' he said in a neutral voice suppressing his irritation. 'Come in.'

'Morning your reverence. It's cold out,' she said a little stiffly.

Without glancing in his direction, she carried a steaming jug of hot water and emptied it into a basin on a marble-topped washstand. Beside it she placed a white towel. She then stooped over the fireplace, rattled a poker amongst the embers which flared into renewed flame and clunked some more coal on the greedy flares of heat.

Featherless old hen, he thought peevishly, watching her thin bent shoulders and the sour rigidity of her lips as she left the room closing the door behind her. He knew he was not liked in the parish, but it was a dislike always shown to him with politeness and that would suffice. He took pride in his unmarried self-completeness, the comfortable certainties of a warm bed, starched table napkins and a smoked hock-joint for his Sunday dinner. He was free from the mundane cares of abrasive reality. He grimaced as his intestines gurgled silently. Throwing back the bed covers he swung his legs off the bed and broke wind which afforded him immediate relief. He padded his way to the heavy brocade curtain. Drawing it back a little he discovered with slight dismay that the world was engulfed in an opaque cold fog, the first of the season. The grass was drenched and he could not see beyond the sombre dripping trees outside his window as far as the little grey church. He hoped the fog would not turn to rain, that would discourage even more from hearing what he so badly wanted to say to them later in the morning.

Turning he caught his reflection in the mirror. The Reverend James Joliffe was a small man and his skinny legs below his night-shirt were as white as candle wax. He lathered his face, stroked the open blade of his razor back and forth along the leather strop and shaved himself fastidiously, unconscious of the vertical frown marks, the weak but sensuous mouth. He felt the top of his head with his fingers feeling for the bald spot which privately so distressed him. Bending his head to the mirror he examined the pale circle of white scalp before carefully brushing a quiff of dark hair backwards over the embarrassment. He felt better when buttoning up his Sunday black and his self-assurance was fully restored once he had adjusted the back stud of his stiff white collar.

Ann Mason lifted her grey eyes to the grey-white fog searching for the source of the sound but the birds were hidden from her view. A chevron of geese perhaps was passing high above the fog in the windless air. She was on the quieter path beside the willow-edged stream which she could hear but not see in the whiteness and she held her child closely in the woollen shawl to protect her from the heavy drips falling from overhanging branches. The mud was as sticky as honey and her boots made the sound of a generous kiss each time she lifted them. It was not a pleasant morning. But rumours were rife that Reverend James Joliffe was going to speak of the disturbances spreading through the counties and she wanted to hear him. It could be important to Joseph. And while they were better off than most the future was uncertain. If they ever fell upon the parish, it would be James Joliffe who would decide their case. It was best they be seen in his pews on a Sunday, and that Robert should continue to sing at his services. He had left before her to practise with the men who formed the small church choir.

The leaded, pale-grey roof of All Saints loomed into view, its single square tower invisible in the still mist. Little Eliza drifted off to sleep as Ann found a place in an unaired corner which held the accumulated odours of wet stone. Conscious of the warmth she held in her arms, she looked at the sleeping face, the closed sandy-lashed eyes, the pert little mouth, and felt a pang of tenderness that misted her eyes. Reverend James entered and the congregation stood. She could hear Robert's strong tenor voice with the choir coming from above and behind her. Ann then noticed in front of her and a little to her right the weather-reddened face and broad shoulders of Deacle encased in his Sunday broadcloth. Unusual for him to be there on such a morning and alone – very! And just off the aisle was Joseph Carter! She drew a deep breath as if she had just escaped some small danger. Carter was a picture of alertness. His attention was fixed on the Reverend James Joliffe. His whole face listened, the tightened lips, the open nostrils, the naked, vigilant eyes. A vague visceral uneasiness stirred within her, intensified without clarification. She found herself searching for Henry Cook. But no! Never! She remembered the early morning knock at her door, the rabbit freshly gutted and partially skinned for her, moisture still clinging to its fur. He knew Joseph was away. Eliza stirred, stretched, but slept. Thoughts, wishes, images continued to jostle in her mind until she suddenly realised that she had heard nothing of the service and that James Joliffe was climbing the shallow, winding stairs to the pulpit. There was a cough from somewhere in the gallery, a shuffling of feet on the stone floor. Communal waiting. Public silence. James Joliffe stood silently for several moments. His hands were joined piously with the tips of his fingers resting on his chin as if praying. His eyes were closed. Lifting his head at last, he surveyed his silent congregation. The sermon began.

'I am about to address you, my friends, on a subject of great importance to us all and I pray you to listen attentively to the advice I most sincerely offer to you. Perhaps you have heard of the change of government in France. The discontented people of that country have forced their king to flee. Will such violence bring peace and security to the French? It is doubtful. In all events, the people of your class will reap no good from it. For the evils which existed, affected none but those far above them. So long as the sun and moon endure, there must be rich and poor. We are all equal in the sight of God. But on Earth there must be, and ever will be, inequality.

'Let us now turn to our own country which you have rightly heard is the richest nation in the world. But what has made her so? Why chiefly her machinery. I have myself travelled in other countries where machines are not so much used and the poor there are worse fed and worse clothed than in our own country. In some parts of France the poorer classes all wear wooden shoes. Would you like to wear wooden shoes? I am sure you would not. Yet every day brings us some fresh account of violent men wantonly destroying property of their employers and neighbours. What country is this to live in, if a man's property is to be destroyed at the whim of every selfish person who would bring all men to a level, not by raising himself, but by keeping everyone else down? You have not disgraced yourselves by such acts in this parish and I rejoice in your good sense, but leaders have been discovered amongst you. Men in the receipt of decent wages the greater part of which they spend at the beer shops where they use their influence in exciting discontent and fanning it into a blaze!'

Ann shifted uneasily. Her anxiety returned this time tinctured with fear. Was Joseph in some sort of danger? Eliza had woken and was becoming fretful, but she dare not leave. She jogged her up and down gently on her knees. No playful, distracting hand was offered to her. No reassuring smile given to Ann. The tension in the church was palpable. It was in the stillness, in the silence. No one moved, no one coughed, no one whispered. Blood filled the veins in the throat of James Joliffe. He breathed deeply and with a visible effort controlled his anger. He continued with a measured intensity.

'That there is much distress is a truth well known, but the cause, I fear, arises from circumstances which no human means can entirely remedy. And yet, who thrust themselves forward to decide these intricate and important questions? Not the wise, not the experienced, but the hot-headed and the ignorant! Lawless rioters who are as learned as the horses they work with! To accuse the rich of being the direct or indirect cause of their poverty is as malicious and wicked as it is false. Do away with machines and tithes, and make landlords lower their rents. This all sounds very well at first but who will then help the poor man in his difficulties? Who will provide for him in times of illness and misfortune? The prosperity of the rich is essential for the welfare of the poor.

'Discontent is the sin spreading like a weed through the

country. Corn has been destroyed! It is impossible to find words strong enough to express the wickedness of such an act. We are taught from our earliest childhood, and most properly taught, that to waste a piece of bread is a sin. If it is a sin to waste a single piece of bread, how great, how dreadful is the sin of destroying in one moment what might support a hundred families! And for what purpose? Is this the way to help the labourer? Will this make his bread cheaper? If ever a man can be said to cut his own throat, surely we can say this of the corn-destroyer, this burner of ricks – Thou art the man!

'Threshing machines have been broken. Why these should be the objects of your disapprobation more than the horse, the wagon, or the wheelbarrow, I cannot tell. I have thought deeply, I have read widely, and I am of the firm belief that machines are a blessing to the rich man and the poor man. It is true that at first such machines put people out of work, and they must find their means of support in some other way. But greater benefits will come in time. Before printing presses were invented all books were written by pens held by the hand and some people gained a livelihood by doing so. But look at the consequences. Thousands now tend printing machines. Before the printing presses there were not four Bibles in this parish; and now, I speak below the mark when I say there are four hundred. Is this not a change for the better? I could give you a dozen such cases. Look at the spinning machines. When these were invented all the spinning wheels stopped in the country and many an honest woman lost her employment. But what followed? You would scarcely believe your eyes if you saw the thousands of persons who work with the spinning frames in Manchester and Stockport. Children as young as nine are gainfully employed in warm factory rooms.'

As if to confirm this truth a watery sun broke through the torn mist and melancholy fog of the morning and the coloured windows of the church flowered and bathed the nave in coppery light. The Reverend James Joliffe smiled. Ann did not like what was implicit in that smile – the touch of malice, the sense of self-satisfaction, the hard uncharitable charity. She felt a profound need of Joseph's calm presence and wished him home. She had heard nothing of him since he had left for Brighton with the petition and its many signatures largely collected by the Deacles. Nearly a hundred and seventy of them, mostly crabbed and uncertain, some merely a wavering mark.

'What need I say more?' James Joliffe's voice had lost some of its stridency but was still unpleasantly over-emphatic. 'Surely you will not suffer these wicked people to gain ground amongst us. We are Englishmen, and above all Christians. Be content! Learn to bear your lot with resignation in the sure hope of eternal justice. Remember as a child you were taught to say, "My duty towards my neighbour is to love him as myself." That I should, "Order myself lowly and reverently to all my betters", and "Honour and obey the King and all that are put in authority under him." Do not risk an untimely, degrading death, summoned into the presence of your maker with a load of guilt to meet the punishment of everlasting misery. We all live by each other – the higher classes in society by their liberal expenditure give employment to the lower classes; the lower classes by their labour give income to the higher classes. We all have our several stations to fill. We must adapt our ambitions to the arrangements of a society which it has pleased God to organise on his own interesting plan. We shall be sure to fare better for it in the end; for what says the Psalmist? "I have been young, and now am old; and yet saw I never the righteous forsaken, or his seed begging their bread."'

Outside the church every leaf sparkled wet jewels in the late morning sun and the few pale smears of cloud seemed to make the blue sky bluer. But there was not the usual genial hubbub. Ann too, felt edgy and wary. She had no wish to speak to James Joliffe and was relieved to see a well dressed, big-bellied man swagger up to the preacher, shake his hand and congratulate him noisily on his sermon. She did not know him, nor had she seen him in the church. He must have been in one of the private pews. She again wrapped Eliza up in the shawl, snuggled her against her shoulder and as soon as Robert joined her, they walked quickly through the churchyard onto the puddled road.

'Get out of there! Go on. Get!'

A dog yelped painfully and fled guiltily from a gap in the hedgerow where a group of parishioners had gathered around what she took at first to be a bundle of rags. Farmer Deacle had dismounted and had left his horse unattended in the road. He bent down and picked up another stone which he pelted at the dog which still skulked nearby reluctant to leave its find.

'Get away with you! Go!' shouted Deacle again.

Her pulses beat more quickly and her breath came hard. It was not rubbish or rags – it was a man. Joseph Carter kneeled at his side. It was a dead man, so wet he may have been just pulled from the water. His black hair and long beard were sticking to his pale wet face and lank jaws – the sightless eyes were open. To her horror Ann saw a small, crab-like insect crawl rapidly across the dead wet face. Carter pulled the corpse a little further from the hedge where the man had sought in vain to find some comfort from the night. The head bumped and fell to the side a little. The open eyes looked at the sun.

'Shall I fetch Reverend Joliffe?' Ann asked. There was pain in her expression. She turned to see the minister shunt the lower bolt and close the heavy double oak doors of All Saints.

'No,' said Deacle with a bitter laugh. 'It will be a behind-church grave for this stranger. Better to fetch the surgeon, I think. Send one of the lads.'

'I'll go,' said Robert firmly, and wheeled away immediately, his face pale and sombre.

A small wet leather bag lay beside the poor wretch. Carter, his big rough hands visibly shaking, loosened the draw-string and emptied the contents – a few sorrel leaves. Carter met the eyes of Deacle in mute sadness.

'Aye,' someone in the group offered, 'even grass by the roadside be a little like bread, it is said, in its taste.'

Ann gave one broken, dry sob. Her brow ached. Farmer Deacle looked her quietly in the face.

'Go home, Ann. We will tend to things here. Take the little one home.'

She looked down into Eliza's face – the wide eyes and little chin. It was monstrous that the years would destroy such perfection. She turned her back on the dead, as the living must, and made her way homewards. The old lady would be worried. She must hurry. The sunken sightless eyes would stay with her. She must have passed him in the fog beside the hedge on her way to church. She prayed that the dog had not been there then. It was the brutal casualness of it that troubled her. A man far from home – a harvest man perhaps – tired and confused with hunger, dragging his steps towards the hedge. A life of detail and circumstance of which she knew nothing reduced to a few rotten grave boards hidden from the world.

POLITICAL REGISTER, 3rd OCTOBER 1830 TREATMENT Of Men Applying for Parish Relief

*F*OR ME, THIS *has been a subject of observation, complaint and remonstrance for more than ten years. The poor rates will, if this system continues, soon bring all the farmers and tradesmen in the agricultural parts, completely down. Let us, therefore, understand the matter.*

I know the country people well; and I know that they will not lie down and starve quietly, and God Almighty forbid that they should for they have been brought, by degrees, to greater and greater suffering. I have seen men harnessed like horses and drawing beach gravel in Hampshire and Sussex. The leader worked with a bell around his neck. I have seen men robbing pig-troughs in Yorkshire; eating horse flesh and feeding from the grains-tub in Lancashire. Men who have three pence a day allowed them in Norfolk. All over England, men, women and children are worse fed than felons in gaols. They know there is no hope for them.

It is madness; it is not error, but real madness to imagine that the thing will mend itself; and it is madness just as complete to ascribe the distress to any but the one cause. That cause is an attempt to collect nearly sixty millions in taxes annually in money of full weight and fineness. The taxes must be repealed and this will never be done effectually without a reform in the people's House of Parliament.

For a long while men will submit until the suffering is so great that life becomes not worth preserving. Last winter they touched that lowest point. Nothing will make them touch it again. Unless radical measures be adopted, and in time too, this will assuredly be the end. Unless this thing be seized upon at once, and wisely and manfully dealt with, our country is doomed to experience all the sufferings of a convulsive revolution.

William COBBETT

5

'WHY IS THAT country clodpole still waiting about in the hallway?' asked William Rowe tersely as he entered the room. Secretary and smallish cog amidst the baffling wheels of royal officialdom, he offered no other greeting as he took his place behind his desk.

Rowe's assistant looked up from a parchment, removed his spectacles and replied sarcastically. 'He is one Joseph Mason from the illustrious village of Bullington. I am sure you know it well. He would like our King to change the law on several matters pertaining to wages, taxes and tithes – if that is not too much trouble – while our sovereign is holidaying here in Brighton. He has a letter or petition or some such thing to that effect which he would very much like to present to His Majesty. It is signed by shoemakers, sawyers, butchers and other sundry bacon-eaters so it carries some weight.' He smirked mockingly while pursing his lips. 'He has been waiting for hours and will not be put off.'

'Won't he now,' muttered Rowe with torpid indifference. He combed his fingers through the thinning marmalade coloured hair above his flabby face. 'We shall see.'

Mason, tall, lean, angular sat half recumbent in the uncomfortable round-backed chair opposite what he took to be a narrow service doorway. Smartly dressed servants carrying trays, folded linen, dusting cloths, buckets – two men brought forth a large gilt-framed tapestry – passed through the passageway. But no one else waited in the hallway with him.

And no sound other than a single peal of fat laughter came from the other door he so wished would open. He had been directed and redirected. He would wait. His nerves were strained and on edge with smouldering vexation and impatience. He waited. And he waited.

It had taken the best part of four days to walk the sixty miles to Brighton along the dusty, dead ground of rutted roads. He had spent the first night in a shabby public house in Langrish near Petersfield. Sitting at the poor dinner placed before him a thimble-rigger entertained some local men. Three times a man who looked like a shearer had successfully chosen the thimble with the pea under it. All the while another man sitting near the scarred doorway and dressed as a shepherd preached unhappily against the vice of gambling. Mason was sure he was in league with the swindler. He carried a heavy cudgel and at his feet was a brute of a dog that no shepherd would tolerate near his flock. 'Go on! Go on, John,' urged the young shearer's companion. 'Ye have the eye for it!' The shearer risked half a crown – and lost. Risked a further sixpence in his desperation and lost again. The bulky shepherd chided the victim for not heeding his sage advice. The man who worked the thimbles sank a pot of dark ale, gave a good hard belch and turned to Mason urging him to try his luck. Unable to detect the transitions of the mysterious pea, Joseph suspected a trick by which it had been removed and was no longer under any of the three thimbles. He was about to say so when he saw a hard quick look exchanged between the thimble shark and the shepherd who rubbed his bony nose with a meaty fist. His dog stood and growled an ugly growl through its wet mauve-black mouth. But Mason's money given to him by the good people of the Dever villages for his journey may as well have been in an iron-clad safe. He would neither be cajoled nor intimidated.

Nevertheless he was pleased to leave in the morning after

a restless night and a breakfast of oatmeal porridge of small measure with both money and head intact. Discouraged by the experience, he had slept soundly in the straw of a barn the following night a mile or two from Pulborough. Wrapped in the single blanket he carried with him, nothing had disturbed him except the distant bark of a dog somewhere and the rough scuttling of rats on the old oak rafters above him. The cold autumn-wind was knife-sharp under a sky the colour of dishwater late on the third day. He was footsore and weary. He had emerged from dark yew and beech woods and onto a chalky down that stretched ahead of him. He could see the white path he was on for two miles or more meandering in round-cornered zigzags up an open distant slope. Nothing presented itself except a modest farmhouse and a ruined barn half a mile above it. It was a poor hen-scratched sort of place. The farmer, about the same age as Mason with a large family, at first demurred, but his wife would have none of it.

'The world's before us yet,' she said squarely to her husband, 'and it be an awful thought to think it possible that we might ever be without a roof over our heads.' The farmer acquiesced with a pleasant shrug of the shoulders and raised arms. 'I'll make a bed up for ye in front of the fire and ye be welcome to it,' she said to Mason.

In the morning she brought in tea, sugar and bread for breakfast and when she saw Mason's blistered feet she set off for a tub of water, a darning needle and worsted and put a kettle on the hob. Mason bathed his feet in the hot water and drew the needle and wool through the blisters – the best possible cure for them. On learning the reason for Joseph's journey, the couple stubbornly refused any payment for their kindness.

'Now for Mr Jack Donkey,' drawled Mr William Rowe indolently as he lifted his weight away from the desk. He had kept Mason waiting a further two hours. Adjusting the lapels on his bulging yellow waistcoat, he ambled to the door with sluggish movements, opened it and beckoned Mason to come to him. He was feeling a cavity in an upper tooth with his tongue when Mason stood doggedly resistant in front of him. They remained in the hallway. Without a word he put out a hand for the papers Mason carried. He opened them peremptorily, glanced for a moment at the fine dame school copperplate that Mason had laboured over and casually tossed them back to him.

'Now this simply won't do,' he said. 'Such a document can only be accepted by the Home Department in London. I suggest you take it there and that is an end to it. Good day.'

Mason stood there fierce and silent. The words knifed into him. Choking back his anger, he stared into the dour, implacable face of William Rowe. It was he realised, futile to argue against such self-centred smugness. He was defeated. He turned on his heels and walked away bitterly remonstrating with himself that he had not uttered a single word after waiting so long to do so. Before he left the building, Mr William Rowe gave a loud sneeze that sounded like some exotic tropical bird. He had failed. His journey had been for nothing. He muttered a quiet stream of invective as he made his way down the cobbled streets towards the sea leaving the Indian domes of the Royal Pavilion behind him.

'If I had but a ha'p'orth of courage,' he said, full of angry self-recrimination.

He passed people, their eyes unseeing. His heavy lace-up boots, coat of fustian and corduroy trousers rendered him invisible to the respectable and the refined. Women in bright colours, with skirts wide and full strolled with men in elegant walking shoes, tight pantaloons and bulging waistcoats. They exuded a contented lassitude as if to silently announce that the measure of a man's mind could be accurately gauged by the length of his coat tails. He reached the sea, a metallic silvery grey expanse in the afternoon light. He stood near some exposed rocks wet with strings of lime-green weed and filled his lungs slowly through his nose with salt-laden air. The slap of small waves on hard-packed sand; the scurry of wave-drawn pebbles calmed him. The shore was alive with the stir and cry of birds. Large gulls squabbled and flapped in the smudged grey light tearing at scraps of broken shellfish. Mason grimaced. All living things it would seem had learned to snatch and gobble, quickly, before another did. And as for people, if the prize were great enough they would tear each other to pieces if need be to reach it. London. It was as far again as he had already journeyed – another sixty miles at least. Impossible with the few shillings he had left. He watched the afternoon light turn a pallid lemon behind a cloud-darkened horizon. A cold wind began to play along the beach. His cheeks marbled in the chilling air. He would go home.

THE BRIGHTON GAZETTE, 6th NOVEMBER 1830

*O*UTRAGES IN KENT: *The county of Kent is in a very agitated state, on account of the organised system of stack-burning and machine breaking which appears to be established in several extensive districts. The farmers flattered themselves that the large rewards offered, which wisely included establishment elsewhere, would have the effect of inducing some of the incendiaries to betray their accomplices, but in this respect they have been disappointed. Recently, several corn-stacks in the neighbourhood of Ash and Lyminge were burnt to the ground. One of the sufferers had boasted that if the incendiaries came to him, he was prepared to meet them with a bushel of bullets. They, however, did come, and his bullets did not save his corn-stacks.*

The High Sheriff of the county, Sir Edward Knatchbull, and Reverend Mr Price succeeded in arresting the ringleaders and in dispersing the mob. But not before one rioter said: 'We will destroy the corn-stacks and threshing machines this year. Next year we will have a turn at the parsons; and the third year we will make war on the statesmen. We will do anything rather than endure such a winter as last year.'

For his active part in the affair, the Reverend Price has subsequently had his ricks fired.

Threatening letters signed with the mysterious name of 'Swing' have been received by many farmers and landowners. Frightful anarchy has spread in their wake and Sir Robert Peel has stated clearly that he will adopt any measure that can promote the suppression of the outrages.

What will such a state of things as this end in? Mobs have scoured the country around Maidstone, parading a tricolour and a black flag. It appears that the conspirators do not seek plunder of any kind but demand half a crown a day as wages. On the 30th of October the magistrates went out with a body of thirty-four soldiers to meet a mob of four hundred people. An excited landowner, mounted on horseback, sent a servant to retrieve the ear of a rioter which he had slashed off. He proposes to mount it in his hall with foxes' masks and other trophies after duly registering it in his game book.

It has been reported that disturbances have now spread to Sussex and it is believed that Sir Robert Peel has ordered two pieces of artillery to be dispatched.

6

JOSEPH CARTER LOOKED up quickly at the sound of heavy boots on the sanded floor, his eyes sharp as splinters in the wrinkled tiredness of his face. His features softened as he recognised the dark hat and figure of Henry Cook. They had not seen each other since the Radical and Musical Society had met at the Swan when Enos Diddams had pleaded for patience until the results of Joe Mason's petition were known.

'A cold morning for this time of year, Joseph, and no mistake,' said Henry, throwing a glance around the corner alcove of daub-and-thatch of the farm outbuilding where Carter was sharpening stakes used in the making of hurdles. Thatching-spars, billhooks and reaping hooks of varying sizes, a bow saw, a discarded field-flagon and lengths of timber lay about in neat disorder. The drawling of hens could be heard from somewhere nearby. Dressed in a leather apron, Joseph continued to sharpen the stakes, placing each in a large wooden vice and with deft movements of a two-handed draw knife he produced a sharp triangular point. The stake then joined a growing bundle by his feet. He paused and looked out at the lonely colour of slate roofs and slate sky. The light fell cold on the wet ground.

'Ees, ees, i' faith, it promises to be a winter as fearsome 'ard as the last.' He stooped and gathered chips and shavings of wood and fed them to a struggling fire which gave off crackling, staccato sounds and the clean self-assertive smell of wood smoke. The back of his left hand was bruised. Its grape-hued ugliness was perhaps the result of a misplaced mallet blow or a piece of flying timber.

Cook looked about him almost furtively. They were alone.

'Joseph, the petition has come to nought. You should have seen the wretched state of Joe Mason's feet when he came home. The man walked for days and it has come to nothing!' Soured by the failure, a profound discontent gnawed at him. He looked directly into Carter's eyes. 'I hear there's been another meeting. Are there plans afoot?' There was doggedness in his voice despite the softness of his tone. 'Were you with them, Joseph?'

Joseph waited a moment nervously before answering.

'Oh, ees, I wor with them. And not agin my will neither!' he added, growing more sure of himself. 'Joe Mason read the letter which came out of Newton to us all. There was no name to the letter. But Joe said he knowed who it came from and Joe is a good scholar. The letter, I know, came from old Diddams.'

'So it's true!' said Henry, feeling curiously elated. 'We are to do something at last!'

'There was much high talk about bringing people to their senses, them in their dandy houses with their dandy habits. That it wor their own fault 'cause they wor too high and must come down.'

'But the letter, Joseph, what did the letter say?'

'I never could read none; no reading nor writing. But I was at the reading on't. It said we was all to leave off work; and the Sutton men was to go out and stop the ploughs. They was to send home the horses for the farmers to look after them themselves, and was to take the men with them. And they was to go and turn the men out of the barns. And they was all to go and break the sheens as the farmers had got to do the threshing. That was what they was to do.'

Henry Cook felt his chest thicken and forced himself to draw in steady, placid breaths.

'When is this to be, Joseph?' he managed to ask. His voice was a razor passing through cloth.

Joseph's voice, when it came, was as faint as smoke. 'Thursday. It be Thursday next week. Word would ha' travelled by then accordin' to Joe Mason.'

7

'ROBERT!' SHE CALLED quietly. And again a little louder, 'Robert!'

He turned in the narrow lane and saw Margaret.

'Margaret? Why are you out here in the cold instead of going up to the house? What's the matter?'

She was well muffled against the cold, but her long dark hair was free. Whipped by the weather her complexion was high. Her bright face was pretty, but she was on edge, vulnerable. She had none of her usual pert egoism and light-hearted banter. He impulsively reached out for her and felt her warmth against him. Her face became contorted, close to tears. The wind surged and wailed above them but compared to the leaden ugliness of the open fields the tunnelled lane fortressed by high bare-ribbed trees was all protected warmth. He bent and kissed her, gently, very gently. They parted and she managed a tremulous, uncertain smile.

'I don't want you to go with them tomorrow. Please!' Again her emotions rose to the surface. There was fear and defiance and petulance in her voice. 'I know I'm silly. I just don't want you to go. I don't want anything to happen.'

Sighing, he put both his arms around her. Her head rested soothingly against his chest. The force of her concern was plain and it aroused a feeling of gratitude in him.

'Nothing is going to happen! There will be a bit of noise and a lot of brave talk.' He deepened his voice in mock intimidation redolent of Old Testament vengeance, 'Money or blood!' He laughed. The emptiness of the threat was clear. 'The farmers half expect something like this.'

She held his gaze. Her face simple and frank.

'For me, please. Don't go.'

He winced in momentary confusion.

'I have to. I have little choice now anyway.' He hesitated, tried to gather his thoughts. 'I'm sorry.' The silence became sullen. 'Margaret, to obey willingly, always to obey, to always accept things as they are is a deadly foe, an awful weakness. I don't want a lifetime of pulling up other people's weeds. I want some sort of future – for us! And the men look to Joe and me. There's no one else.'

8

IN THE BLANCHED coldness of early morning, Joseph Mason had a final lingering look in the small dusty mirror which hung from a peg in the wall. His face was grim and creased. He was growing old, he thought, introspective, a little morose perhaps. He carelessly rinsed the razor in a basin of soapy water already cooling into a grey scum on the washstand. He had passed an anxious night of intermittent sleep. He had dreamed. Straining upwards to the surface of morning consciousness had brought with it the lingering sensation of broken teeth. He could still feel, as if it had been lived experience, his mouth full of brittle shards.

There were sudden shouts, confused and excited, and the discordant blare of a horn or an old army bugle. Here already!

'Joe, they are waiting for us. We must go,' said Robert striding past him and out into the unbright light outside.

Ann stood at the threshold, one hand raised to her mouth in apprehension at the sight of some forty men who had gathered in the garden. The clothes of some were falling almost to rags; others stood in bedraggled and tattered smock frocks and mud-clogged boots. Most had the pinched, wind-burned complexion of men who spent their time in the open. They carried wooden stakes, grub-axes, a pick handle. The Sutton blacksmith rested a sledgehammer over one ample shoulder. And Henry Cook was there. He carried no weapon. One man at the head of the phalanx of noisy men brandished a gallon loaf of filthy bread impaled on a pitch fork. Under the dark mass of his ragged beard, the Stratton man's hard-lined face was whey-white from hunger.

'Where are ya, man?' He shouted with rotten gums. The bread danced on the ugly fork underlying the bitterness scored deep into his being. 'Join us or have ya back chalked for a deserter!' His face was twisted and ugly as he yelled.

Words formed and beat on the border of Ann's mind but she remained silent. Joseph went and touched her face with his hand, his thumb lightly caressing her lips. Eliza began a sudden wailing cry from her cot in the next room.

'Goodbye, Ann,' he said simply. He pulled on his heavy outdoor coat and reached for his hawthorn walking stick from its place behind the door.

She nodded almost imperceptibly, 'Goodbye, Joseph.'

Ann watched him walk to the men who quietened at his approach. Joseph Carter came forward to greet him. His face shone with excitement.

'Such a mob you never seen before, and if you live for a hundred years, you never will agin,' he said, looking younger than his forty-five years.

'It will be bigger yet by the time we visit the penny-pinching farmers of Micheldever,' encouraged Joseph, appealing to the group with a clear rising voice.

'Barton Stacey first, surely,' said Robert, 'a short visit to Reverend James Joliffe who preaches so eloquently against the poor!'

Hoots of agreement came from the men and another burst of sound from the horn leapt out into the windless air.

'We are for Borough Farm, Robert. But some men go with Robert, if you please. We will meet at Stratton or Sutton this afternoon.'

'Ann, see to the child!' Old Mrs Mason's querulous voice asserted itself above the rowdiness outside.

Before closing the door, Ann saw the men divide into two groups. Joseph set off without a backward glance with Henry Cook at his heels.

The Reverend James Joliffe was seated at his desk in a warm-coloured room overlooking the flint-walled churchyard. He placed his steel pen into a stone ink jar with a flourish. He was pleased with his work. He gently pushed a cup of old bone china further away and brushed some crumbs off the leather writing slant with a finger tip. He was rummaging in a brass handled drawer for taper and wax to seal the letter when he heard loud ragged voices rising outside. A shiver of apprehension ran through him as he opened a small-paned window and looked out. His housekeeper, Mrs Ashby, confronted some twenty men across his garden gate.

'What do you want?' she demanded fiercely.

'To come in,' was the sullen reply. 'We want to speak with his Reverence.'

'Well you can't,' retorted Mrs Ashby, not without a touch of malice. 'I've just locked the gate.'

There was a brief moment of silence shattered by mocking jeers and yells of disapproval.

'He will be spoke to!' came a voice as a man wearing a filthy rust-black coat stepped forward from the crowd, raised a pick-axe and smashed the garden gate open with a blow that sent it slamming savagely against the stone wall.

James Joliffe's face was the colour of canvas. He couldn't breathe. His chest was a cringing, shuddering turmoil. His bowels turned to water. He tried desperately to steady himself against his desk as Mrs Ashby pounded up the stairs and, without pausing, ran into his room panting like a mastiff.

'They are at the door and calling for you,' she blurted out.

His mouth was dry, his tongue a brass clapper in a broken

bell. His eyes blurred in his almost exhausted breath. The sound of a muffled, crude laugh climbed the stairs to torment him. 'I can't,' he stammered. His voice came out in lumps. It was as if words had become solid objects he could not dislodge. His weak chin visibly trembled.

'Hurry, you must see them or you will have them in the house,' she insisted. Her voice was little more than a whisper.

James Joliffe lurched unsteadily towards the door knocking over the stone ink jar as he did so. The ink stained the green leather desk top with the saturated darkness of wine or blood.

He stood before them.

'How we have waited for you, sir,' Robert Mason greeted him with a grim mocking air. The sarcasm was extreme. 'Pondering your text for next Sunday's sermon perhaps? Can I suggest "Those that work shall not eat, and those that do not work shall have food!" How I know you gentlemen with your glebes and tithes!'

'But, but – I am a friend of the poor!' fell from his mouth in a dead voice.

'Then you will gladly make a donation of five shillings to us the poor of these parishes,' said Mason, smiling icily.

There was a scuffing of boots and murmurs of approval from the men, most of whom had unthinkingly removed their hats in the presence of the clergyman.

'Five shillings. I, I don't have five shillings,' said Joliffe, rallying a little from his distress.

'You have it and we want it. We have been living on potatoes for long enough and now we must have something better,' demanded Robert.

'We can work as well by night as by day,' someone said sourly from behind Robert.

'Damn your black blood – no money! We will go to work now!' threatened another.

'I will pay! I will pay!' retorted Joliffe petulantly. He disappeared into the sanctuary of oak floors, the glow of red firelight and chintz covered armchairs.

Robert Mason's voice trailed after him. 'What says the great St Paul? "And now abideth faith, hope, charity, these three; but the greatest of these is charity."'

'You will rue this day – grieve for it,' muttered Joliffe with considering eyes as he dropped the coins into Mason's large workman's hand.

'Thank you for your charity so freely given,' he said triumphantly. But Joliffe's words had penetrated him like a dull sting.

Joe Mason and the men with him left the road and trudged towards the farmhouse through nettles powdered with frost. Smoke mounted faintly skywards from the chimney into a morning as clear and sharp as cider. A streak of movement burst silently from frost-bitten bracken ahead of the crowd of men. A hare! It tore away swerved and zigzagged frantically across the open field of stubble to disappear in brown stillness. Joe Mason and Henry Cook caught each other's eye. Both smiled.

William Paine had been waiting and saw them coming. He left the kitchen, closing the door on its rich aroma of baking apples, to meet them in the dreary muddiness and hen-cluck of the yard. He stood askance, large and fleshy, in a low-crowned hat, legs apart, taciturn and inert – and waited for them. Joseph caught the movement of a woman's face at a sash window set in weather-stained stone and scarlet splashes of Virginia creeper. He took in the little garden of fading Michaelmas daisies, the naked branches of a plum tree scratching at the sky, a gingham dress drying on a hedge.

'And what might you be wantin'?' His voice had an edge of

challenge. He stood in silent opposition to the coarse, care-worn faces before him.

'An advance of wages to two shillings a day for your workers,' said Joe Mason unflinchingly, 'and we want to break your machine.'

A shuffling muttering of approval came from voices behind Mason.

A pause of some moments lengthened into a tense silence. Chatter from a knot of sparrows in a nearby thatch seemed to emphasise the quietness. Paine pursed his lips. 'I suppose so,' he said, full of resentment. 'Two shillings a day I consider reasonable. Two shillings a day it is, if other farmers will.' William Paine was not a man to smile, but he nodded. 'And I will seal the bargain with a gift of beer – now, but my machine must not be broke, for I have not used it to the disadvantage of any man's labour.'

Some of the older labourers in the crowd nodded and murmured in agreement. The Sutton blacksmith, his heavy hammer clenched effortlessly in his meaty fist, was stirred to speech.

'Aye, let it be, he's been a man all said and done,' he said through missing teeth.

'No, damn it all!' exclaimed Cook, his dark eyes glazed defiance. 'It must be broke along with the others.'

He came forward and met with no resistance as he took the hammer from the blacksmith and strode off with it in the direction of the barn. A whistle and cheers went up for him and other young workers followed him. Rounding a corner, Cook startled a ewe which fled in a scatter of black dung, and a workhorse growing impatient in its stall shook its neck. It stood in the damp pungent odour of stale urine and piled manure. Cook opened the ancient wooden doors of the barn. The boards of the floor were rough and uneven. A large grain sieve was leaning against a wall beside a wooden cannikin. Flails lay about in silent abandon. He filled his lungs with the clean smell of chaff and grain. The stillness and cool air were unnatural in a place where the resounding slap of the swinging leather flails was usually heard from morning till night; where men worked in open shirts wet with sweat oblivious to the winter cold outside. And there, beside sheaves of barley, was the machine which took their work away, which left them idle and hungry.

The blacksmith's hammer had a handle of ash two feet long and a head of forged steel which weighed six pounds. Henry raised it with the full force of youth and delivered a shuddering blow to the side of the threshing machine that sounded as if Paine's old carthorse had forgotten its gentle nature, had shied and kicked the machine with his huge iron-clad hoof. But surprisingly little damage resulted.

'No. No,' said a youth who had entered the barn behind Henry. 'Its guts are on the other side.'

The next blow of the hammer, and the next, were into the teeth of a series of iron cogs and connecting levers which twisted and fell solidly onto the floorboards raising dust and scattering grain. The sound left behind an intense silence. Satisfied, Cook turned and joined the men in the yard.

'Now if ye'll take the advice of a fool,' said Joseph Carter to Paine, 'ye'll pay for the work we have done for 'ee this morning and we'll disturb you no further.'

Cook stood at Joe Mason's side, his chest heaving with the throb and flow of blood from his exertions. He held the sledgehammer in both hands.

Paine glanced a forefinger against the grey stubble of his chin. 'I have but a sovereign in my pocket,' he replied sullenly.

There was a glint of gold which slipped like a fish

between Paine's fingers into the proffered leather bag Carter produced.

Joseph Carter glanced at the sky – nearly midday. He listened to the leap and hiss of dry hay stubble against his trousers as he walked across the field. How much money did he now carry? Robert Mason's mob had rejoined them, and others from Stoke Charity had fallen in as well. He was now with over sixty men. More! After Paine's farm they had visited Richard Deare – one pound; then Thomas Dowden's place where they had insisted upon two pounds as he had most land. At Twitching's another two pounds. He carried all of the money. 'Because I be honest,' he said quietly under his breath. 'I be honest.' He smiled slightly, a mere tightening of the skin. There must be thirty pounds or more. Nearly two years' wages! The mob reached the London road and headed north along rutted cart tracks towards East Stratton and Sir Thomas Barrents' mansion. Heavy boots lifted the dust. Beside him trudged the East Stratton labourer who had spoken out at the Swan. He still carried his pitchfork and stale bread. Carter saw his bone-thin wrists protruding from the frayed cuffs of his coat and heard the rasping intake of his breathing. The man was tired, or ill. Spit had dried white in the corners of his mouth.

Interlacing cries and a clatter of hoof beats made Carter look behind him. The London coach. It had slowed at the sight of so many men on the road. It drew alongside him. The teamed horses sweating and straining; the coachman in an oilskin and broad-brimmed hat; a woman passenger was beside him, her close-fitting bonnet tied with black ribbon; the lanky guard swayed in his dirty scarlet uniform. Ah, it'd take but a moment to shimmy up onto that coach, Carter thought. Me with me thirty pounds and get away from this whole business. He started forward a step or two – hesitated. And what's to become of me poor wife? And what a vagabond they'd all call me! There was a throaty 'Har!' from the driver, a slap of reins and the coach was gone.

'Hark forward, go at it! Beat the iron to pieces!' urged the Stratton man. His pale eyes glittered feverishly from the shadowed cups of wrinkled flesh. He felt a sharp stab of excitement. He could hardly find his breath. His rough-wattled neck gulped and quivered under his matted beard. The mob had surged like a wave into the high-roofed barn belonging to Francis Callendar of East Stratton. Sir Thomas Barrents' colossal white mansion nestled in woods and parkland a quarter of a mile away. The noisy tumult and clamour of movement suddenly stopped. Men parted, fell quiet. Francis Callendar, steward to Sir Thomas Barrents, stood before them caught in the dappled-dustlight of the barn. Tall and stringy with bunched shoulders he was wearing riding boots, bright with polish, a twill shirt and a plum-coloured foul-weather coat. He looked as clean and supple as a cat amongst the rent and ragged assemblage of men around him.

'It's Callendar!' an anonymous voice snapped out.

'Who wants him?' retorted the steward truculently. He turned with a cold hard expression in the direction from where the man had spoken.

'Captain Swing wants him!' came sardonically from further back in the crowd.

'We have done our work well,' said Cook standing by the broken threshing machine, 'and we will be paid for it!' He saw the flicker of recognition cross Callendar's face; the strained intentness of his grey eyes.

'Five pounds,' demanded Joseph Mason. 'You gentlemen

have been living long enough on the good things, now it's our time and we will have them.'

'Or we'll smash yer windows for 'ee!' someone cried out stridently.

'Five pounds,' said Mason again. 'Don't cavil at it man. We cannot live on our wages.'

'I refuse!' The words were not spoken loudly yet conveyed a stubborn vehemence. A weak tint of colour had appeared in Callendar's face. 'And that's the end of it!'

There were protests, snarls, whimpers. Someone in the mob tried to speak, choked, hawked phlegm up out of his throat and spluttered, 'The end has not yet come! That will end in blood,' he almost croaked.

'Down with the big house! We'll set the bloody place on fire!' the Stratton man almost shrieked. He threw his pitchfork violently to the floor in impotent anger.

'We must have money or we will do mischief,' said Mason warningly.

'Well, don't do mischief,' said Callendar abruptly. 'I will speak to two men in the house. Two only.'

He turned on his heels and braved his way out of the barn. Joseph Mason followed with Carter at his side.

Callendar faced them, formally separated by a gate-legged table, in what was the morning room where the steward was accustomed to work. Behind him was a desk and a mesh-fronted bookcase which was mostly devoid of books but had bundles of papers tied in pink ribbon on its shelves. Wood lay across iron dogs in a small, unlighted fireplace. A long-case clock ticked solemnly.

'This is an extraordinary demand,' Callendar said, visibly nettled.

'Ten pounds? It's none too much,' replied Mason soberly, 'if your windows are to be spared. And if I am to turn the mob away from Barrents' house.'

'Sir Thomas is in London. There are none but the housekeeper and servants there,' complained Callendar. 'It would be churlish…' He broke off hesitantly. An edge of desperation had entered his voice. He stared with a fixed intensity at Mason for a moment or two, and then inclined his head grudgingly. His hand entered his breast pocket and brought out a thin wad of crumpled notes. He selected one written for ten pounds. 'Here is your money!' he said cuttingly, his eyes bright with anger as he handed it to Mason.

The men had waited outside Callendar's garden. The small iron gate gave a sharp clack as its spring drew it shut behind Carter. 'Ten pounds!' he shouted waving the money above his head. Three cheers were raised.

'Now to the nearest public house,' said Mason, 'where every man will have his half pint duly paid for by Mr Francis Callendar! Carter, here, will keep count of the beer that is drawn.'

Another cheer – pick-axes, pump-handles, sticks and different kinds of tools were raised in salute. As the men moved forward towards the road, there was the sound of a horse from behind the house. Callendar, his face clouded with silent fury, was urging his black gelding to a gallop, but not in the direction of Sir Thomas's mansion.

Late afternoon, rooks crossed the sky. The Dever River slithered and side-slipped along beside them appearing and disappearing among wind-ragged bushes, winking and flashing in the last of the sun. Inky, blue-black shadows cooled in the encircling dusk which presaged night. Joseph Mason was walking home with a dozen men a league or so from Bullington. Long shadows advanced in front of them. Henry Cook, his black hat decked out with laurel leaves, plodded contentedly beside him. He still carried the blacksmith's hammer. Together they savoured the day's triumphs.

'Promises made and bargains struck,' Joseph said in a satisfied voice.

They smiled broadly at each other. Mason put his arm around Cook in a quick affectionate gesture. A wage increase to twelve shillings a week for married men and nine shillings for single men had been promised to them by one Dr Newbolt, an alderman and magistrate from Winchester, in front of a huge crowd at Sutton Scotney – provided that the men dispersed and returned to work – a promise readily conceded to. Thirty-five pounds collected by his own mob had been equitably divided amongst the participating parishes in a meadow before leaving Sutton. Thirty-five pounds!

The man in front of them stooped in a patch of mottled shade to acrid dead leaves and slipped a fallen chestnut out of its bulging spiky burr. Straightening, he lightly tossed it into the air and caught it in the palm of his hand. Muted laughter came from behind him at some gentle ribaldry. Was it Carter? Robert Mason tramped in meditative mood some half-dozen paces behind the group. So, it was over. Suddenly, the man holding the chestnut came to an abrupt halt. 'Hello! What's this? Gentry,' he said, his face troubled. 'I didn't know Barrents had an interest in the poor.'

Bingham Barrents, nephew of Sir Thomas Barrents, stood in the middle of the narrow path in front of them. They became aware of Bingham's men moving out of the shadows behind him.

'Who is in charge here?' he demanded in a voice louder than was necessary. His heavy squat body in a coat of Prussian-blue, a white cravat and topped with a heavy felt hat loomed incongruously in the half light. 'Who is your leader?' he asked a second time, his mouth sneering at the word.

'I am,' said Joseph Mason forthrightly and came forward.

Barrents seized him. Immediately both groups fell upon each other. There were the muffled thuds of fists on flesh and the uneven gasps and grunts of great exertion. Henry Cook's strong-veined hand tightened on the hammer he carried. He tried to push towards Mason but found himself off balance and held by the wrists in a grip of steel. 'God damn you, get out of my way!' he cried with fierce resentment. Something savage and irrational welled up from the depths of his being. Galled by months of pent-up fury, he twisted in a frenzy to free himself from his opponent. He saw the sudden fear in the man's face. He could smell the sourness of his breath. Jerking his left hand free, his fingers brutally tore at a hank of hair forcing the man's head back. He retrieved some leverage and the man heeled over sideways – his face fish-pale. A hand went up to the blood and spit dribbling onto his chin. Cook did not even know his name.

The men now stood like spectators around Barrents as he struggled to restrain Joseph Mason. The two parted, staggered, and tried to regain their balance. The hammer, as if of its own accord, leapt from Cook's hand. The blow glanced off Barrents' hat and shoulder and the hammer landed with a dull sodden clump on the ground behind him. There was a moment of heaving silence, of stillness. Barrents, but little hurt, was helped to his feet by his men. It was over.

Cook was beside Mason. 'Joe, are you hurt?'

For a moment his reactions were slow and clouded. His coat sleeve was torn along the seam at the shoulder, but he had received no blows. Cook's eyes, wide, needle-bright with tense alarm – and fear – met his. The incident and the sense of shared but ineffable knowledge drew them for a moment together in a complicity of silence.

'I'm all right Henry. I'm fine.' But he was left with a lingering unease of things not yet fully understood.

They left the shadowy edges near the trees and made their way across springy grass tussocks without further challenge. Henry Cook's self-absorbed face was pale and dewed with perspiration. He could not control the sudden trembling of his hands. There had been nothing between the moment and... Barrents lumped on the ground. He walked on in an aching, constrained silence. The ebullience of his earlier mood was gone. A nagging fear that would not be assuaged had replaced it. He turned, his attention drawn to a lone horseman on a nearby hillock with the last of the dying light behind him. He instantly recognised the black gelding, the high black riding boots. The rider wheeled his mount in the direction of the coppice they had just left.

9

FOR ANN THE day seemed of immense length. She moved through the dragging routine of her work in a distracted mood. She felt anxious and strained. She knew that the tight knot of worry twisting inside her would not loosen until Joseph had returned. Her agitation and impatience were obscurely transferred to Eliza who was fractious and irritable all morning. Her talk with old Mrs Mason was awkwardly cheerful, a little brusque and impatient at times. The child and the old lady now slept. The cottage was silent and asleep. It, somehow, resembled her strangely. It was nervous too. Its quietness was aimless rather than peaceful. It held a menacing, unnerving quality. At times she was curiously frightened, as if her happiness had somehow been wrestled away from her. She felt utterly alone. She sensed prophetically that she must conquer the feeling, that if she could not, a fissure deep within her would open and she would be lost. She needed Joseph with a desperate urgency. The endless day slowly wore itself out. She left the house, glanced at an unclouded sun setting in a pallid sky. A light faltering breeze died into windless calm. The chill air became glassy and sharp. He must be home soon. She slowly walked along the path towards the road that would bring him back. The memory of Henry Cook striding off with Joseph that morning came to her and cheered her a little. There was something touchingly gentle even diffident in the boy's devotion. Her dark unsettled mood would soon dissipate she knew with their return. There would be good cheer, mugs of cider and contentment around the fire.

She saw Joe.

His face, strained and exhausted, looked strangely blank. He had not seen her. When he did his face softened with sudden relief. He opened his arms to her. They hugged each other fiercely. He held her arms, gently cupping her elbows in his strong hands, and kissed her softly on her forehead. Something had shaken him badly.

'Your coat!' Frowning, she caressed the torn material at his shoulder with a light almost shy touch. 'Where's Robert? What have they done to you?' She was close to tears.

'Robert is with Margaret. He said he would be home within the hour.' There was agitation in his voice. His face was grim.

A sharp pain of fear stabbed at her. 'It's Henry, isn't it? Something has happened to Henry.' Her voice quivered like a struck string.

Quailing inwardly with a violently felt guilt, he looked at her with softness in his eyes and nodded.

10

HENRY COOK LAY in the darkness of his small one-roomed cottage in the empty hours of the night. He slept but fitfully. Anxiety gnawed at him. There had been no pursuit. Little harm had been done, after all, a few blows exchanged – no more. Perhaps Barrents would leave it at that. But his mind would not settle. The moment of the hammer leaving his hand came back to him over and over again. The memory of Barrents slumped on the ground, cringing and shuddering, tore at him and filled him with dread. It came on waves of nausea and bitter regret. It haunted him like a spectre. Should he flee? He could travel across country and be miles away before dawn. But where would he go? He was a poacher by descent and was not ashamed of his father who had taught him the skills which put meat on the table. He admired in himself his ability to be independent and generous when he was able to be, but away from his familiar haunts how would he live? No hearth would welcome him if he left the valley. Here he lived alone but was not lonely. The life of the vagrant was no life at all. He knew such men, their faces worn with raddled veins and eyes as empty as the road ahead of them. Lips flaked and broken, racked by hollow coughs, beards matted in clumped straggles, plodding onwards in the hope of a day or two of slavish, animal drudgery, ditching or dredging gravel with a hand-scoop. Once, with his father, he had seen three men fighting. They were giddy and wild. They stumbled about and yelped in high voices, desperate to claim ownership of a filthy bundle of rags that was once a coat.

His thoughts came back to what preoccupied him – Barrents.

Again he was gripped with a deep sense of foreboding. For weeks he had been fiercely anxious for action but now all was spoilt by that one ugly and unlooked-for moment in the copse. He would go to the Masons in the morning. Joe would know what to do. When his father had died he had gone to Joe. It had been there that the wall of his grief had broken in a flood of wild shuddering sobs. It had been Ann who had held him in her arms until his despair was mute. It had been Joe who had saved him from returning to his cottage and to what lay there cold and lifeless under the covering of an old blanket. Yes, he would go to the Masons. Joe would know what to do. His aching restlessness calmed and faded into exhaustion. He slept. Images drifted unbidden to the surface of dream consciousness. He was in an unfamiliar street. He could not find his way. People and places came to him in seamless chaos. He was both participant and spectator. Nothing surprises the dreamer. He stood in woods shadowed and sombre. Felt the weight of something heavy in his hand. A sense of unease congealed into fear. He tried to run but was weighted down and could not. He could not move his heavy limbs. He grunted with the effort. Woke. Starting at a half-heard sound, he turned on his side and saw a handful of turf-fed fire glowing drowsily in the rusty grate.

He began to sweat. The close fug of the hovel oppressed him with its unpleasant smells of smoky tallow and fusty thatch. He felt shut in, stifled, trapped. He was close to sickening panic. Throwing off the coarse heavy blanket, he drew on his laceless boots and went outside. He carried a large pannikin to the rain barrel. He struggled briefly with the lid; its wet woody smell competed with the sharp-scented mint growing at his feet. He filled the pannikin and drank the cold water. He slowly breathed in the clear chill air of the night. An owl floated softly out of black trees to hunt the frosted fields under a wasting moon. The stars were chipped ice in silent sky. He still held the lid. Its wood was as smooth as a sea shell, as familiar to him as the snaith of the scythe. No. He could not leave this place to tramp the roads to certain death. What would Joe Mason think of him if he were to disappear without as much as a word of explanation or of farewell? It was cold. A shiver ran through his shoulders. He returned to the crumpled abandonment of his bed. Slept, dreamed again, before waking abruptly, jarringly as a wine-yellow glow was spreading on the horizon and the first notes of birdsong emerged from the dimness. Light leaked into the room through the small chinks in the wall.

He left a kettle on the hob and walked into the blown cloud of his misted breath towards the ditch which served him as a privy – and froze. Not ten yards away behind a stunted holly bush stood a soldier. His musket was trained steadily on his chest.

A voice, sharp-edged and high-pitched rang out from somewhere behind him, 'So much as take a step Henry Cook and sure as God you will lie dead in that drain.'

He knew the voice, Barrents, Bingham Barrents! Damn him! Damn him! Blind fury surged up within him making him light-headed. His chest swelled and fell in extreme agitation. Another soldier materialised from the shadows carrying heavy iron handbolts. His jacket was as red as smeared blood.

'Give him your hands, you scum!' ordered Barrents who now came forward with a third soldier by his side.

There was no escape. Begrudgingly, he did so. His arms dropped under the weight of the irons and he felt the rough smoothness of the metal cut into his wrists. Barrents walked in front of him, to and fro, his face paled and his lips tightened, quivered slightly, before they slowly gathered into a smile. Suddenly, he hit Cook across the face with the full force of his open hand.

11

'AND TAKE THIS.'
The voice and the eyes held no apparent emotion. The man held out a cake of cracked yellow-white soap. It filled Joseph Mason with revulsion. Someone had already used it. It was wet and soft in his hand, like something living. The man bundled up his clothes on the rough bench in front of him and gestured curtly towards the washroom with a toss of his head. Mason could feel the grit on the flagged floor under his bare feet. There was a strong odour of damp wood and wet weathered bricks. He carried the coarse material of the prison uniform and the soap towards the shivering cries of men forced to wash.

They had come for them in the afternoon, two newly sworn in special constables whom he did not know. All had been sudden, rushed, there had been no violence, no altercation of any sort – no time to say goodbye to Ann. He was left with sharp, disquieting images of men with reddened, wind-swept faces and broad shoulders; one sullen and mulish, the other with an expression both tense and teasing. And of Ann, standing in the doorway crying, her face gaunt and troubled, with one hand raised in melancholy salute, while Eliza stared in quiet puzzlement.

Joseph and Robert Mason followed the square bulk of a gaoler along a hard, narrow corridor. He stopped at a door fastened with a chain at the top and one at the bottom. Both were fixed to a peculiar shaped piece of metal like a large corkscrew or a pig's tail. There could be no escape from such a place. The man selected a heavy key from a rusting wire ring and turned the heavy lock. They stepped into sudden darkness. The door to the cell was closed behind them with a solid, iron-hard sound. It was as if they had entered the confines of some primitive, savage cave. Large black distorted shapes lay twisted on the floor in front of them. Some of them began to move. The air was close and heavy with a mixture of odours. The acrid sharpness of carbolic could not completely mask the dreadful sourness of sweat or the close stench of the waste pail. Their eyes began to adjust to the darkness. Men were lying on the floor sleeping or trying to sleep. A spare white-haired man shuffled crab-like to his left making a little space for them. They put the chaff-filled mattresses they had been issued with on the floor. Robert sat down and gathered the blanket he had been given around his shoulders. Its coarse, furry texture gave him little comfort. He groaned audibly and began to choke. It was the smell of the place. He struggled to stifle a rising sickness.

'Ye'll be better in the mornin', the old thin man beside him murmured coaxingly. The flesh had fallen from the bones of his face and hollows like caverns had opened around sunken, rheumy eyes. 'They'll let us out into the yard in the mornin', ye'll see.'

Sick at heart, Joseph lay on his back and listened to the soft babble of voices around him. A low fierce mutter vowed to mark the men who had detained him. 'Damn their eyes!' he cried, suddenly shrill. 'And their sheens,' another doggedly added. The night quietened into desultory whispered talk. He was grateful that no attempt had been made to separate him from Robert. And clearly the regulatory great silence imposed on all prisoners had completely broken down due to the overcrowding of the cells. Rueful exhaustion slowly stole upon him disordering his thoughts. He remembered the crowds at

Sutton Scotney, their shouts of triumph. Many had thrown their hats into the air wildly cheering. It had only been yesterday! How could so many have been taken so quickly?

'Poor men wanted work. I do not blame this on Mister Cobbett. I ha' nothing to say agin he.'

It came from out of the darkness with a slight sharpness of irritation in it.

Joseph sat up recognising the voice instantly. 'Joseph Carter!' he exclaimed.

There was a moment of bewildered silence.

'It be he indeed, Joseph Mason. Is that Robert with you?'

'It is,' said Robert plaintively.

'Who would ha' thought? Good God that ever this should be! And Cook. Henry is here as well somewhere. I seed him when I wor brought in but ha' no chance to talk to him,' said Carter in a softer voice.

The talk of Henry returned Joseph to those moments of frenzied chaotic motion in the copse when Barrents' men had attacked them. He could see Henry, his face distorted with physical effort and filled with confused angry distress trying desperately to reach him, to protect him from Barrents. He felt an immediate sickening sense of guilt. Surely no harm would come to the boy. But he could not dismiss his anxiety as imaginings. A sudden anguish gripped him at the idea of Henry suffering because of him.

The cell door opened with a clatter of chains. A gaoler stood holding a lantern; its frail light flickered in a halo of yellow fog. Shadows and half-shadows moved over the man's ill-shaven, pock marked face.

'Joseph Carter,' he demanded. His voice was authoritative and deep.

It was as quiet as a stone. The stillness palpable.

A coldness came to Carter's stomach. His arms felt weak.

He rose stiffly to his feet, frowning with anxiety and deep confusion. 'My name be's Joseph Carter.'

'You are to come with me,' said the man turning towards the cell door.

Joseph Carter followed the threatening figure. The gaoler said nothing further but led him some distance to another section of the prison and to a smaller cell. Carter glimpsed walls that had once been painted a milky-green and mustard yellow, but had darkened to grey. There was a bench for his thin mattress, two wooden pails, one empty one full of water, and a cake of yellow soap. The door closed behind him with a dull clang and he was left there alone.

I URGE ALL *landowners and magistrates to put yourselves on horseback, each at the head of your own servants, retainers, grooms and gamekeepers. Fortify your houses. Arm yourselves with horsewhips, pistols, fowling pieces and what weapons you can obtain. Attack in concert, or if necessary, singly, these lawless, rampaging mobs. Disperse them and put into confinement those who do not escape. Hunt down their leaders. Seek them out. Take them from public-houses, cottages, stables and outhouses where they may attempt to hide. Arrest all those tainted with the stench of the radical. Do this and our country will once again be tranquil, and that in the best way, by the activity and spirit of gentlemen.*

Despatched from the Duke of Wellington in Hampshire

12

'As I said, I know the man well. I have done work for him. The two of us will be sufficient, but I will need a carriage.'

'Hire one, but don't go to much expense,' said Bingham Barrents. 'Here is the warrant. And take some handbolts with you.'

William Lewington, saddler and harness maker of Winchester, and newly sworn in special constable hesitated.

'Handbolts? Surely that will not be necessary.'

'I insist on this,' said Barrents in a sibilant rush. 'I want the man in handbolts!'

Mrs Deacle, a little woman with a grey shawl about her head, stood in the cold light of the yard throwing grain to the hens from a cracked china bowl. They dipped and swerved about her feet with an excited cluck-clucking competing for her largesse. Her face was gaunt and grey. There was darkness under the eyes. She was tired, desperately so, and laboured under the yoke of illness. She breathed in the whole gamut of farmyard odours, as she surveyed the greyness of the morning. Falls of rain hung in curtains from a bruised dark sky to the north. The east was shining polished pewter. Fitful gusts of wind tugged at her shawl; fretful thoughts tore at her mind. She was afraid. The Mason brothers had been taken. Henry Cook had been paraded before a troop of soldiers to Winchester goal. Joseph Carter too – gone from them. Her hands moved in a pathetic, helpless gesture. The hens squabbled and pecked at the last of the grain.

'Giddap!'

She started. Their three collies barked and moiled about a small, unsprung cart as it tilted and jolted its way towards the house. Its wheels rolled, angled and spun as its driver urged a grey pony along the road which was as rough as a ditch. It was Lewington. He was fond of their servant, Ann Scarlet. But what on Earth possessed him to visit in an old cart and on such a day as this. Then she saw, some three hundred yards behind the cart, a heavy man on a large brown bay. She did not know him. She hurried to the house, entered the kitchen and her day fell in ruins.

Lewington nodded and muttered a greeting. Her husband, dressed in a shooting jacket, sat at a scoured table under old dark beams eating bread and cheese. His gun rested against a wall. A rabbit, beginning to stiffen, lay draped over a large earthenware dish, its eyes fixed and glassy. Ann Scarlet put the kettle on the hob to heat.

Lewington's face reddened. 'I have a warrant against you,' he said, then broke off uncertainly.

'Let me see it,' said Deacle calmly looking him in the face. He took the blue document and read it. His thick stubby fingers tapped noiselessly on the surface of the table. 'The magistrates must be mistaken,' he said, 'my conduct has been the reverse of that imputed to me. I walked with no mob. But sit down, take some bread and cheese and I will go with you.'

'Mrs Deacle must come too,' said Lewington flatly.

'Mrs Deacle is very poorly at present,' said Deacle almost gently, as if to remind Lewington of his past associations with the house.

The dogs which had been lolling and panting on the flagstones at Lewington's feet suddenly started up and gave a peremptory bark or two. Mr Bingham Barrents now stood behind Lewington. He eyed the width of the farmer's shoulders – the gun against the wall.

'Constable, do your duty, handbolt him!'

With a suppressed exclamation, Deacle began to stand up, changed his mind and sat down in stony silence after giving out a long hot sigh.

Lewington turned the key in the spring lock of the handbolts. Barrents instantly began a tirade of loud weighted insults.

'No, you didn't march with the mobs, you whop-straw, but you and your missus here walked the parishes to put signatures on Mason's bumpkin petition!' His lip curled with spiteful venom. 'What's that if it is not aiding and encouraging the mobs? You are a traitor to your own kind. You…' The sentence petered out. A man carrying a shotgun was standing at the door. Barrents drew a pocket pistol from his coat and went to the man. The octagonal barrel of the loaded pistol aimed at the man's head. 'Put the gun down!' he almost shrieked. The man did so immediately, his eyes bulging.

In the brief eternity that Barrents' pistol was aimed at the man's head all that remained was for the shot to ring out, the volley to reverberate and echo crashingly around the room. Ann Scarlet was crying, a low harsh weeping. She made no effort to wipe her crumpled face.

'Don't be a fool, man!' said Deacle sharply. 'He is one of my men. We have been out rabbit shooting.'

Barrents glowered at the workman. His mouth pursed. He lowered the pistol, and then stooped to pick up the shotgun. He took it to a large stone ewer near the old-fashioned windows and poured water into it to render it lifeless.

'Don't spoil my guns; there is no necessity for it,' said Deacle. 'Good God! Nobody here is going to use them. I am innocent of this business.'

'Get him into the cart,' Barrents ordered Lewington roughly.

Ann Scarlet raised her apron to her face and knuckled her

eyes. Deacle stood up and walked out to the cart without a word. The grey pony stamped a hoof impatiently. Mrs Deacle sat with her head bowed. Her eyes brimmed with tears.

'I cannot go in the cart,' she said, 'The roads are so rough. I am too ill. Let me take my own horse.'

'Get her in the cart,' shouted Barrents, struggling to control himself. 'Or do I have to do it myself!'

Lewington caught Ann Scarlet's look of silent condemnation. Her eyes still streamed. Her face wasted. Behind her the kettle boiled. Its lid clattered and water splashed and hissed in the flames. He shook his head. 'Good God, sir, let the lady have her horse. I will be answerable if she goes away.'

Barrents turned to the man who had held the gun. 'You will put her in the cart,' he demanded.

The man's eyes flashed anger below a frayed straw hat. 'Not I, by God! Not if me life depended upon it!'

Barrents placed his still-loaded pistol on the table. Moved to the diminutive figure of Mrs Deacle, placed one arm behind her back, another behind her knees, and lifted her bodily from the chair. She winced in pain, but did not call out. He strode out of the house and almost flung her onto the rough, dirty boards of the cart.

The cart lurched. It shuddered and jarred its way to the road. From there, it was six miles to Winchester. They passed through light sweeping showers of cold rain. Their breath misted. Mrs Deacle moaned and begged Lewington to go more slowly. Her voice was choked and muffled. She made an attempt to get out of the cart. Deacle put out an iron-ringed hand to her.

'Sit still, my dear, it is better to be quiet.'

Upon this, Bingham Barrents rode up beside them.

'Sit down, damn you!' he cursed.

There was a sharp hiss of the riding crop falling. He hit

him across the face, across his mouth, so viciously that he fell immediately half-stunned. A gout of blood spurted from his broken lips, from the beat and throb of sudden pain. His face was a numbing cold fire. He paled in anguish. His eyes ran with water – not tears. A little runnel of blood ran down his chin. He bored a sidelong glance into Barrents' retreating figure.

'We must be quiet,' he said in deep distress to his wife. 'For now!'

THE JOURNAL OF LADY BARRENTS 1830

*T*HE MONTH OF *November began inauspiciously in spite of the popularity of the King and Queen. The King's going to the House and his return was hailed as it ought to be, but the Duke of Wellington was greeted by an angry crowd who hurled stones at him! The new police so recently established to replace the old and useless watchmen were set upon by the mob aided it would seem by all the thieves and pickpockets of London. Many were badly hurt.*

As the month advanced it became increasingly gloomy. A universal spirit of dissatisfaction seemed to pervade every class. The good harvest did nothing to lessen the murmurs of discontent. Riotous mobs rose very unexpectedly and spread with alarming rapidity breaking threshing machines, extorting money and demanding higher wages. Why I cannot understand, for wages have been the same for several years. We were informed by our nephew Bingham that on the 19th not only were threats issued against Stratton Park, but also that his very life had been placed in mortal danger when he confronted an armed mob! We promptly returned to Hampshire. Nightly patrols were established to defend the house and Sir Thomas took to sitting up at night convinced spies from the rioters still lurked in the grounds. They must be able to bear the cold like cattle!

The Special Commission established in consequence of the riots came to Winchester on the 18th of December. Entering the county, the judges were greeted by a procession headed by Lord Salisbury. The Sheriff, gold-chained and in his brocade, rode out from

Winchester with a phalanx of liveried javelin men, his tenants and servants, his outriders and his two bannered trumpeters. Our own Bingham Barrents followed leading a cavalcade of nearly two hundred special constables to do honour to the judges. The procession extended a full mile. The bells of the cathedral and city churches pealed out as the judges' coach, flanked by the javelin men, rumbled its way up the steep High Street through the ruined west gate to the venerable Great Hall. The judges dismounted from their coach and entered by the narrow door in the flint walls. The Crier called for silence and the commission of the Assize was read before proceedings were adjourned. The judges, Baron Vaughan and Justice Alderson dined with us afterwards and we had a large party besides, numbering sixteen. River trout, roasted partridges, apple charlotte meringue rounded off with fruit complemented tirades against that 'damned scribbler Cobbett', 'the Jacobin fog drifting across the Channel from France with its contagion' and 'the taint of radicalism' in the villages that had to be assaulted with unwonted terror and severity to restore the foundations of the social order. The whole business of the trials was finished within a week with only one capital conviction after reprieves and commutations. Nine baronets, four knights and six Members of Parliament sat on the Grand Jury. The judges when they travel the country certainly go through it en prince.

Our Christmas was passed quietly at Stratton Park. The Yule log was burnt in a large hearth. The peacock in full plumage was placed on the dinner table, with, of course, the boar's head. The immense candles were covered with laurel. The hare appeared with the red herring astride on its back and the claret was not inferior to last year!

13

HENRY COOK, POACHER and squatter's son, stood in the dock and peered up through the dimness of the December afternoon towards the bewigged figure of Baron Vaughan, high on his throne beneath the panoply of King Arthur's table, jury to the left, magistrates to the right, bathed in a dim light and the glow of judicial scarlet. The Clerk of Arraigns was embarked on a chilling incantation... *and that the said Henry Cook, being an ill-designing and disorderly person, did combine with a riotous multitude armed for plunder in defiance of the law, and not regarding the pains and penalties therein, did on the nineteenth day of November of this year wilfully attack the gentleman Mr Bingham Barrents with the intent to murder him...*

The scriveners wove curlicues endlessly around those few moments of panic and fear in the near darkness of the coppice, transforming the shambling crowd drifting homewards that evening into anarchists and investing Cook's deed with a deadly malevolence. Henry could barely stand. His strong legs were straw. They trembled under him. The dark, lofty columns of marble and the sombre high-pitched roof of Henry III's Great Hall oppressed him. He was faint. The crowded gallery of faces pressed all around him; they leered and jigged and swam in distorted liquid images of noise. He was filled with anguished desire to be outside in the open air away from the accumulated vicious savagery which lay hidden behind the fine clothes and formal words of the speakers.

'Prisoner at the bar, how do you plead? Guilty or not guilty?'

Cook found the degree of attention almost unendurable, but some crude power within him rose up in a deep swell of unthinking energy. He clenched his fists. A flash of hate was in his eyes.

'Not guilty.'

He said it with little forethought, not knowing it was the same response which John Body and John Slade, both Hampshire schoolmasters, had made in the same ancient place when they refused to accept the Queen as head of the English church in 1583. They were hanged, drawn and quartered in the towns where they lived. He did not know that in the same Great Hall it was the response of Sir Walter Raleigh condemned to death as a traitor in 1603, the response of Captain John Burleigh who was accused of causing a drum to be beaten as a rallying call to rescue Charles I from Carisbrooke Castle. Convicted and sentenced to be hanged, he had to take leave of his wife and child in the street outside on the way to his execution. Nor was he aware that here too, the seventy year old Alice Lisle pleaded not guilty but was sentenced to be burned alive for having the temerity to shelter two refugees from the Battle of Sedgemoor. The weight of the past could be crushing in such a place. Only fifty years before Cook stood in the dock, prisoners had been branded, then and there, with irons heated at a fire in the centre of the hall.

'God send you good deliverance,' responded the Clerk.

Mr Bingham Barrents was called to the bar as plaintiff.

'On the nineteenth of November I met a mob of about thirty or forty persons proceeding from Stratton,' he began in a voice of calm civility. 'Some had sledgehammers and sticks. I got off my horse and walked to the mob. I expostulated with them. I then called for their spokesman and Joseph Mason came forward. He told me they had broken machines. I made him repeat the words several times and then I collared him. Before

I could turn around, I was knocked down from behind by a blow between the shoulders. I sank under the blow instantly. I lost my senses for a moment and then found myself in the arms of my own men who had come forward. I should add that the prisoner does not know me and therefore could not bear any personal malice against me but must have acted in the heat of the moment.'

Throughout this speech, Barrents did not at any time look at Henry Cook standing pinched and pale in the dock. He fixed his eyes upon the judge alone with a steady, penetrating gaze.

William Tibbell was called as a witness.

'I was with Mr Barrents on the nineteenth of November,' he said tonelessly. 'I saw Cook come up with a sledgehammer on his shoulder and heard him say, "God damn you, get out of my way." I saw the sledge rise and immediately fall, but I could not see any hand. As soon as I saw the hammer drop, I ran to Cook to prevent him from delivering another blow.'

Judge Baron Vaughan gave an audible sniff which lifted a corner of his upper lip. The fingers of his plump hands were interlaced in front of him. Fattish and balding under his wig, his heavy reddish face was without any trace of discontent. Sanctified by divine service that morning at St Maurice's Church at the foot of the High Street and fortified by a sermon impressively delivered by the Sheriff's chaplain, he sedulously presided over the destiny of those who entered the dock with the assurance and freedom of a god, a Jehovah in ermine and full-bottomed wig, cutting a righteous swath through evil-doers with a decisiveness and despatch felt to be salutary. Nearly three hundred bewildered prisoners, some herded into the dock in groups of more than twenty, passed before him in that week alone.

'What is the prisoner's occupation?' he asked in a voice of keen severity.

'Labourer, Your Lordship,' promptly replied the Clerk, and then added with a contempt that curled his lip into a sarcastic smile, 'and well known poacher.'

Cook, bewildered, stood biting his mouth, his eyes frightened and struggling. He could not bear it. He felt that in a moment he might break out into hysterical gasping like some appalling wild animal. He took a deep slow breath and gripped the railing in front of him. His brain reeling he searched in vain for Joe Mason in the crowd.

'Lay your heads together gentlemen,' the judge instructed the jury. 'Consider your verdict and acquaint your foreman!'

The jury was worthy of Baron Vaughan's confidence. They did not retire and found the prisoner guilty of assault with intent to murder.

'Henry Cook, unhappy man, you stand in the presence of God and your country convicted by a dispassionate jury of attempting to murder Mr Bingham Barrents. To the delicacy of that gentleman you owe much and I should not be doing justice to that admirable man if I did not state publicly that he has done everything in his power, consistent with the oath he has taken to speak the truth, to make the offence you have committed against him as slight as possible. Mr Bingham Barrents having seen a riotous mob armed with sledgehammers and crowbars, and evidently proceeding in a course which, sooner or later, must produce a breach of the peace, had the kindness to call for the ringleader. The mob, however, were deaf to his remonstrations. When Mr Barrents, wishing to protect the property of his neighbourhood, attempted to seize Mason, you called out for the way to be cleared before you, and then were seen to raise the sledgehammer with both hands and to strike at the head of Mr Barrents. That blow, lighting on his hat and the collar of his coat, was so far weakened in its effect as to prevent it from being fatal. But it was still sufficient to bring him senseless to the ground. Even when he was in that senseless condition, you were not satisfied, you were making a second effort to complete your purpose when you were prevented from doing so by the actions of William Tibbell.

'I am satisfied with the verdict that declares that it was your intent to murder Mr Bingham Barrents. Can any man doubt that with such an instrument as you used, if it had fallen where it was intended to fall, you would have occasioned his death and rendered yourself guilty of the crime of murder? Aye, and not only rendered yourself but all who surrounded you at the time, all guilty of the same crime. People ought to be careful how they mix themselves up with illegal assemblies when they are all to be made responsible for a guilty act committed by one of their number.

'And, therefore you, Henry Cook, must consider your life forfeit to the law. You have all the moral guilt of murder on your head, though you happily did not succeed in accomplishing that fatal purpose. It is my bounden duty to mark the prisoner who now stands prominently at the bar, as an example and sacrifice to be made on the altar of the offended justice of this country. Your days are numbered. The gate of mercy on this side of the grave is closed against you. You Henry Cook must prepare forthwith for that great change which now so suddenly awaits you. All interest in the cares and pursuits of this life must vanish. Now you stand before an earthly judge, clothed with all the infirmities of man's frail nature, but you will soon stand before your heavenly judge from whom no secrets are hid and there to render account. Let me entreat you to lose not an instant in soliciting his peace. On leaving this place lose no time in availing yourself of the excellent spiritual assistance that is within your call and hope that even at this eleventh hour your prayers may be accepted.'

Judge Baron Vaughan had finished. He nodded to the Clerk of Arraigns.

'Does the prisoner have anything to say?'

Henry Cook did not lift his head. His face twisted with anguish and became blank, resigned. He shuddered convulsively. He shrank within himself with a sickly feeling of dissolution. He no longer stood erect but slumped. His strength drained away. His fine physique seemed suddenly diminished – less sturdy – some power had been riven from him.

'I proceed to pass upon you the dreadful sentence of the law,' said Vaughan grimly.

He waited impassively. The silence was savage. There came a shuffling of feet behind His Lordship. Reverend Robert Wright, Chaplain of His Majesty's Prison Winchester, had risen and placed the black cap over the wig of the Baron and fussed over its exact positioning for a moment or two before retreating once more.

'Henry Cook, you will be taken hence to the place whence you came, and thence to a place of execution, there to be hanged by the neck until you are dead; and may the Lord God Almighty have mercy on your guilty soul.'

The words fell like dead things. The great iron wheel of terror began to turn. Cook was led from the hall. He moved as if in sleep.

14

H E JERKED AWAKE clutching the rough prison blanket in his hands. A single candle moved only inches from his face. Blinking in the light, Joseph Carter looked blankly at the face before him, the high cheekbones, the hard brown eyes, the severe lips, before his mind surged to alertness in silent panic. Robert Wright, clergyman and prison chaplain, placed the candle on the floor, sat on a low wooden stool and in turn studied Carter's face with a probing uncertainty.

'I have news for you,' Wright said in a tight, controlled voice. 'Cook is to hang.'

The shock was palpable. Carter heeled over and rested his head against the rough stones of his cell. He struggled for breath in the dank still air. His face was drawn and pale.

'He walked with your mob didn't he?' said Wright, giving an odd calculating smile.

'He did. God help the boy!' said Carter. He lifted a grimy hand and rubbed his closed, encrusted eyes with a thumb and second finger. He craved air. Clean fresh air, away from the deep-seated carbolic darkness and the bluntly gross odours of the slop pail. His own body had a dreadful gritty sourness. The candle flame did not waver in the congested stillness. It threw no shadows against the pallid grey and yellow walls. The soothing tyranny of Wright's voice continued.

'And the Masons now,' Wright left the sentence to trail into a thinking silence, but he noticed the flicker of interest in Carter's face. 'It will be the hulks for you my man – or New South Wales.' He looked at Carter sharply. 'Perhaps it won't go so hard for you. It needn't you know. You see, the Commissioners are not really interested in men like Joseph Carter. They want to rid themselves of the real trouble-makers, the ringleaders and organisers. The Masons have been convicted of leading a mob, but are not yet sentenced.' His expression became one of purest complicity. 'I may be able to make things a little easier for you. Can you tell me about the Masons and their so-called Radical Society? Did the Masons do the planning for the mobs? Do they work for Cobbett?' The wheedling tone ended in a patient, contemptuous smile.

Carter did not want the silence that lingered. Why didn't the man go? His pale, attenuated fingers drummed the black cloth of his knees as if he had all the time in the world to wait for an answer. Oblivious to the startling odours of the cell, his face was as clean as an apple, damn him! Now he knew why he had been given a cell to himself! Half-suffocated by the weight of conflicting emotions, he struggled to speak.

'I knows this, an' I'll say no more. I been afeard, but I ben't the least afeard now, damn ye! Joseph Carter may not be much as you say, but he won't split. He won't peach for 'ee and yer fourpennorth of Christian charity. Devil take me if I do!'

Unable to hide his prim disapproval the clergyman pursed his thin lips and said, 'I will come again. I will come often. We will speak of this again.'

He reached for the candle. An almost fanatical look glittered in his eyes. The gaoler came forward and the prison chaplain blew out his candle. All sounds guttered into silence.

15

S WOLLEN CLOUDS HELD snow in a livid grey sky. The thin light was cold and watery, snow-light. Joseph Mason greeted his brother in silence even though he knew the gaoler would not object. They walked with a shuffling gait along Jewry Street towards the Great Hall. Their shoulders hunched against the raw cold. It was the last day of the assizes. Today the guilty were paraded and sentenced in batches. No word had yet reached them of Cook's trial held the day before. Robert took hold of Joseph's arm and held it.

'Have you news from Ann?' he asked. His tone was brittle and joyless.

Joseph shook his head. 'No. Nothing,' he said faintly, sadly.

'We will be home soon,' said Robert, 'a week at most.' He tightened the grip on his brother's arm encouragingly. But he seemed to be struggling to convince himself. '"Sure I am that the Lord will avenge the poor and maintain the cause of the helpless,"' he quoted from his favourite psalm.

Joseph's mouth grimaced into a mirthless smile. 'I have a whole chapter of Isaiah in readiness for the edification of His Lordship!'

Anger, too deep for speech, flickered up inside him at the thought of Vaughan – and fear – and shame. The bitter hilarity and laughter rang in his ears once more. Enos Diddams had had the courage to appear at his trial as a character witness. *It was a petition to His Majesty about the poor. The sovereign people of this meeting determined to send a person up to present their petition to the King.* Open sniggering then laughter came from the gentlemen in the jury. Such language, such pretensions from Hodge, the brother of the ox! The poor clod-hopper! But Enos had persevered. *It was not a petition to raise wages, to break machinery, or about any other political concern. The sovereign people subscribed seventeen shillings to carry the man to Brighton.* Baron Vaughan himself was overcome. He snorted derisively and was forced to dab his face with podgy fingers and a clean white handkerchief. The mockery had lingered in his eyes and in his voice. Now he had to face the man again.

They were shepherded past the broken walls of the West Gate which loomed dark and savage in the leaden winter sky and into the square. In the chill air it was a windless grey wasteland. Groups of waiting prisoners huddled like beggars around a church door. A few stamped their feet. Others tried to rub life into gloveless hands. Some, their faces drawn and gaunt, stood quietly and unresistingly in staring blank abandon. A man with a broad, rough face reddened from the cold lifted his shaggy black head to Joe in recognition. His brow contracted into a heavy frown, his mouth began to work.

'Damn their eyes!' The words came from him as a snarling shout. 'They are going to hang the boy.' He bowed his head a little and knuckled the side of his nose in distress. 'Henry, Henry Cook is to hang.'

Joe Mason stood perfectly still in stunned bewilderment, only his eyes were alive, and they were full of torment. Everything seemed to darken before him. The words drove into him again and again. He winced as if he had received a mortal wound. He saw with a painful vividness Robert's face, damp and bloodless, the hunted uneasiness and the fear in his eyes as if he wanted to acknowledge something but could not. *Henry Cook. Henry Cook was to hang!* The words were unbearable. They were left in the aching emptiness between them. The judges would leave. Three Sundays would come and go. The gallows would be built.

The heavy hand of the gaoler pushed Joe's shoulder. 'Move on! Move on!' he ordered roughly but without malice.

Joe stumbled forward wearily, shaking with shock.

Judge Baron Vaughan raised his voice and grew more animated in the sure knowledge that his comments would be widely reported.

'As to you, Joseph Mason and Robert Mason, you are men in the occupation of land, men of superior education and intelligence who have stimulated others to tumult and riot. You are persons not engaged in husbandry who labour under no necessity and suffer no want which makes your offences of a deeper dye. Let me state publicly that in the course of these trials we have found few instances – I am not certain I could lay my finger on one – in which the pinching spur of necessity has compelled the offenders to the commission of their crime. There is no country where charity falls in a purer stream than this. Let the man make his appeal in a proper and respectful manner, and he may be assured that appeal will never be heard in vain.'

A short silence for effect. The scowl on his soft face grew more pronounced. A tone of keen severity had entered his voice. Now he was Baron Vaughan, practised orator and judge of men.

'Simple labourers have fallen prey to the suggestions and instigations of evil designing persons. The men before you have for months past been actively employed in sowing the seeds of disaffection in the villages. You, Joseph Mason, have been convicted of robbing William Paine and putting him in bodily fear. For the conspicuous part you played as leader in the events of the nineteenth of November, the direction of this court is that sentence of death be recorded without being formally pronounced. The part you took, the share you had in the division of money in a field, and that the said money was raised by forced contributions from farmers under threat of violence, show that you had more to do with the dangerous and outrageous proceedings of that day than you are willing to allow. You must not expect any further mitigation of your punishment other than sparing your life. You will be cut off from all communication with society and be transported for life.'

Here he paused, glanced a moment into the convict's face which was ivory-white. He raised his brows waiting for a response. Joseph could say nothing. His thoughts were in turmoil. He felt ill. He gave himself up to the void encompassing him.

Unperturbed, the Baron continued. 'Robert Mason, you have been convicted of leading a mob to the home of Reverend Joliffe, at Barton Stacey, and by threats and violence obtained the sum of five shillings. Sir Thomas Barrents himself has taken an interest in this case and has prompted the Reverend Joliffe to prosecute as a matter of principle. But taking all these circumstances into consideration, I am justified in thinking that public justice will be satisfied. The prisoner to whom I now address myself is, as I have said, a person moving in a better class, and ought to have set a different example.'

Again he paused and gazed indifferently at his man in the dock. His lined and pouched features were at rest. He appeared to yawn vaguely.

Colour mounted to Robert's face in a blaze of defiant anger. There was something inside him which would not yield. He faced his accusers, his eyes furious. He well understood the charade being played out around him. It was water-clear. He and Joe were marked men. Having some influence in the valley, they were dangerous and must be rooted out. The petition had been a mistake. He feared for those who had put their names to it.

'I have never committed a dishonest act in my life,' he said sharply. 'As to my being present on the occasion at issue, I point out that if the learned Counsel who has painted my conduct so blackly were present at the time and wore a smock frock instead of a gown, and a straw hat instead of a wig, he would now be standing here with me instead of being seated where he is.' His face twitched with anger and exasperation. He saw a ragged group of prisoners who had been brought up from the cells and were next in line for summary justice. He appealed to the blurred faces of the crowds looking up at him. 'Do not be cast down and trod under ever more because of what has happened. There will be a reformed Parliament or a revolution before next summer!' His voice had been strident but he began to falter. His face pale and hostile was the colour of buttermilk. Silence engulfed him. He could say no more.

Baron Vaughan was unflurried. 'Robert Mason, you will leave this country.' His flaccid throat moved. His voice was cold and disdainful. 'You will see your friends and relations no more. The land which you have disgraced will see you no more.' His lip curled slightly – contemptuously, sarcastically. 'New South Wales is a place where there is a shortage of manual labour and little machinery to assist it. That you should have to employ the rest of your days in labour, at the will and for the profit of another is needful to show the people of the class to which you belonged that they cannot, with impunity, lend their aid to such outrages against the peace and security of persons with property.'

16

OLD MRS MASON carefully balanced Eliza over her shoulder and rhythmically patted the baby's back. She did not struggle. Warm and comfortable, she would soon be asleep. And Ann would not be long now. She was in the barn milking the cow. What they all called a barn. It was little more than a lean-to. But there was enough hay to make it as snug as a badger's hole. The old lady hummed softly to the child and looked out the window at cold, slate-grey skies. The clouds held snow that would not fall. Ann would have her forehead against the warm flank of the cow. She hoped the warmth and wet breathing of the animal would have a calming effect on her. They must be patient! They would be home soon. The men in Kent had suffered little for their protests. But there was ice in her soul. She felt Eliza's soft shell-pink face against her deeply wrinkled cheek. Her old eyes swam with tears.

The house felt underused – the bare table, the empty chairs, the dark-wooded sideboard with its few plates. She heard sounds she would not normally notice. The rustling in walls. Thin squeaks and titters. The click of old timber as the cold tightened its grip. The soft pop and collapse of embers as they died. The quiet soughing of her own skirts. Again she was drawn to the window. Ann was walking towards the house. She appeared small and vulnerable under the vastness of the dark ranges of massed cloud. Her gaze was fixed on the frozen shaggy tufts of dead grass a little in front of her feet. She carried a heavy pail and in the crook of her other arm was balanced an earthenware flagon that Joseph used in the fields. The heavy scarf she wore when milking was wrapped tightly around her head. There was a call and Ann's face brightened with alertness. She stopped, placed the pail on the ground beside her. She still held the flagon and waited for the man who had hailed her. Old Mrs Mason narrowed her eyes. It was Mrs Reed's oldest boy from Micheldever. There must be news from Winchester! His chest heaved from running and despite the freezing air he took off his hat. Wide-eyed, his hands agitated and anxious, he said something to Ann. The flagon slipped from her fingers and shattered into shards on the cold-hardened ground.

Snow fell in the silence of the night. Great feathery flakes of it whitened fields and cottages, and blanched the narrow cobbled lanes of Winchester. The sharp ugliness of black slate roofs was snow-moulded into round, white, misting smoothness. Large flakes sailed silently through the air, others wheeled around to fly back up into the darkness of the empty night.

THE TIMES, 8th JANUARY 1831
CONVICT UNDER SENTENCE OF
DEATH AT WINCHESTER
(From a Correspondent)

*T*HE 15TH OF *January has been fixed for the execution of Henry Cook, the unhappy man who was sentenced to die at the conclusion of the Special Commission which was recently held at this place.*

The petition presented to Lord Melbourne and signed by six thousand inhabitants of Winchester, praying His Majesty to remit the punishment of death has failed. It was signed by bankers and every tradesman in the town without exception. Application was made to the clergy of the cathedral for their signatures, but they refused to give them. They told the petitioners, as I am informed, that they would not sign any such petition unless the grand jury and the magistracy of the county affixed their names to it.

Surely, of all classes of society, the clergy is that which ought not to be backward in the remission of offences. They are daily preaching mercy to their flocks, and it wears but an ill grace when they are seen refusing their consent to a practical application of their own doctrines. Whatever my own opinion may be, I am bound to inform you, that, except among the magistracy of the county, there is a general, almost a universal, opinion among all ranks of society, that no good will be effected by this sacrifice of human life.

The gaol governor has ordered the scaffold to be brought nearer the prison wall so that the execution can be in full view of the expected crowds in Stapleton Gardens below as well as the felons in the gaol yard. It has been inspected and approved by the prison chaplain, Reverend Robert Wright.

17

'WE ARE ALL prisoners. Everyone is lonely. But there is a way to find peace. The converting God of grace comes freely to the very chief of sinners. Believe. Believe in Jesus who was God manifest in the flesh. Wash in the blood of the Lamb and all your sins will be blotted out from the book of remembrance. Your soul will live if only you believe.'

Cook had grown tired of Robert Wright's web of exhausted words, his constant clerical nagging, little of which he understood. But he did know that reality was something else. The woods and fields had taught him a more ancient law of life. He loved their fragile beauty but knew too their hard cruelty and vast indifference. He had no memory of his mother who had taken him to church as a little boy, but readily recalled his father's contempt for the sleek black priests with their boyish faces. *Actions speak the truth; words always lie* was his father's gruff summation. Cook began to quiver with the intensity of his feelings. The man gnawed at his strength and tormented his mind. 'I don't believe in your God,' he said in a burst of belligerence, trying to tamp down his anger. There was a short unnatural silence. His chest grew tight. 'When I was about twelve, I saw them bring out a drowned child from the mill-race. The mother took her dead child in her arms and refused to give him up. Did your God in his mercy think that up? He must have known it would happen since before the world began – so we're told. He controls everything.'

The clergyman was unmoved. 'God is mystery through and through,' he continued in a tone of soothing softness. 'We are mere mortals. If we could understand God we would be his equal. We would be God!' He allowed himself an indulgent smile at the prisoner's ignorance. 'The reason he permits misery is that good men have the opportunity of lessening it.' He paused. A sour, unpleasant tone entered his voice. 'I must tell you, the bellman will pass your cell at midnight tonight. The hangman comes for you tomorrow. Believe or you must sink lower than the grave into the bottomless pit.'

Cook drooped before his eyes and the chaplain registered the look of utter defeat with an almost savage satisfaction. They were as silent as prayer for some time before Wright again took up the cudgels of his faith.

'Think of this. I take your hand and hold it over the open flame of this one small candle. How long could you endure it? In but a moment your skin would be blistered and cracked and weeping. Tomorrow you will suffer, and you deserve to suffer, but if you acknowledge your crime and plead for forgiveness you will enter eternal life and bask in the Lord's glory! I can save you!'

He had reduced Cook to a degrading childish terror. He was on the verge of collapse, physically it seemed or perhaps it would take the form of a hysterical rending of the mind. Wright was suddenly unnerved, afraid of the man. He took up his candle and left him in the audible darkness of his cell.

Enfolding darkness. Cook lay on his side on the narrow chaff-filled mattress with his knees drawn up almost to his chest. Unseen above him in the mid-winter darkness the huge ordered wheel of stars slowly turned on its axis. The moon circled, compelled by some timeless instruction, trapped in a slow, unalterable pattern. He was afraid to go to sleep, but drifted off into brief restless moments of unconsciousness disturbed by short nervous dreams that he could not remember. Midnight had come. And the bellman. The cathedral clock struck some hour. He did not want to count which. Three. The present declared itself. Inescapable. Inexorable. He was spared the hells of conscience at least. He had not contributed greatly to the world's pain. And above the stars slow wheel? Beyond the darkness? A God of everlasting fire? Surely the pain of this world was enough. No, there was no God. No magic. No judge. Only the darkness. His tiny cry of pain would be but a sound that broke for a moment on the night and died away, only serving to make the stillness, the silence deeper.

He slept again, an unquiet sleep, and this time what he dreamed he did remember. New snow creaked and crunched under his boots. Sharp lights at night. Tracks. Rabbits. The two rear feet like elongated eyes imprinted in the snow. And between and behind them the forefeet forming a nose and an oval mouth. It looked like a child's mask. Hundreds of these ghostly faces peered at him from the snow. He lifted his gun. But it would make no sound. His brain reeled. He felt himself falling. He jerked awake. How long had he slept? The hangman. He would pull on the victim's legs if necessary. Anguish came on him like a suffocating physical pain. What if he fainted? Would they carry him to the gallows? A muscle on his face jumped with little jolting twitchings. Tomorrow, for certain, he would be dead. The earth. He would lie in the earth. He had played in the churchyard. He had run among the dead laughing. Wind-chewed stones. Slate flaking. Bent. Some wafer thin, the names worn away by rain and time. Lost to silence. There was a sick feeling in his throat and stomach. His breath tore. The life inside him breaking up.

Weeks of drizzling rain and bone-white fog. Damp clothes over a chair that stood back-on to a smoking turf fire that refused to flower in the grate. Frills of yellow fungus appeared. The walls, swollen and mouldering ran with moisture. His father broken by work and weather lay under a woolly huddle of rags. His breaths came in slow, harsh sobs, which hollowed and whitened his cheeks. He was racked with a cough that could not move the suffocating congestion on his lungs. He lay helplessly wheezing and choking – his hands were cold, his fingers twisted and knotted with pain. He heaved in a breath and let it out again all ragged and fractured ready for endless unseen sleep.

He wanted his father. But he could not come to him.

He felt the rough texture of his clothes. He could hear a voice. His father was crouching at the fire. Wood smoke, a clatter of cast iron; he saw firelight flare on strong arms. He was a child. He left the hovel unnoticed and walked into the warm countryside, the path softened by moss and old leaf-fall. The sun poured yellow on the heightened green of the grass. White clouds drifted in a blue sky. The quietness rose and fell all about him. He breathed in the fresh green smell of clover, the scent of warm bark. Insects whirred. Dragonflies with glass wings skimmed the surface of a pool hidden amongst wet bracken. High leaves netted dazzling shafts of dappled light. Cow-parsley whitened the hedges which hummed and chittered with a life of their own, intent and purposeful. Laburnum and broom were out, a mass of yellow. Sun-warmed, he sat hidden in tall downy grass and grew sleepy. Tiny birds, biscuit brown, made quick flits between grass stems.

He was awakened by muttering voices. Two men, keepers with their guns, were not twenty yards away. A large dog was coursing and lolloping about the field with its muzzle close to the ground. It came up and peered at him, its tongue trailing from the hot breath of its mauve mouth. The men stopped, suspicious. One of them, with a large florid face, shifted and coughed. His deep seated eyes narrowed and searched the swaying grass. He gave a short startling whistle and the dog bounded towards him. The boy did not move. He lay in the moulded grass hardly able to breathe. The wind rose. Deep surges went through the grass which undulated above him. In his terror he could not move. He waited. He was safe. He burst into a wild storm of deep racking sobs. He did not leave the grass.

The light began to slowly seep away. The shadows lengthened.

'Henry! Henry!'

His father stood in yellow furze near a stream. He did not call loudly, but urgently. He saw the little boy burst from his cover. His face white as porcelain was streaming tears. He was running towards him oblivious to the nettles on his bare legs and feet. His arms were lifted to him. He took him up. 'All is well! All is well!' he said. He tenderly wiped his face with the rough sleeve of his coat and lifted him onto his shoulders. The sun had set fire to the sky. Fiery clouds seethed with brightness, garnet red and vermillion.

Pallid light seeped through the pale square of the window recessed high in the wall. A pigeon flew to the sill, moved its wings lazily. Then fluttered about madly striking the pane and was gone. He envied the bird. The world outside. Clean air. Pulsating life.

'Henry! Henry!'

Although the words were gentle he started. The air was piercingly cold.

'The chaplain and – they are waiting for you.'

The gaoler was rough but kindly enough. He placed a pail of clean water on the floor of the cell and soap and some rough material beside it. He removed the slop pail foul with the voiding of the prisoner's bowels without comment or grimace.

Cook sat upright on the edge of his mattress. His mouth was sour. He tried to thank the man, but his voice thickened and produced nothing but a guttural noise. Then he was alone again. The back of his hands pricked with fear. He looked up at the empty window where the bird had been. The glass was stippled and filigreed with ice. He listened to the suck and draw of his breathing. Felt the rhythmic flow of blood through his heart. The pulse still jumped in his face. He folded his arms onto his shoulders and felt the heavy knotted strength there. But his strong body was a thing of fragilities: fragility of bone, fragility of nerve, of breath.

He moved to the water and took off his old greatcoat, his shirt, and the corduroy breeches. They would all go to the hangman, even his battered boots. He reached down, scooped up a double handful and splashed it over his head and face, shuddering and gasping at the icy coldness of it. It was snow-cold, brutal. Clean. Again and again he bent to the wooden pail. The water shivered and showered over him. It spilled in strands down his shoulders spattered onto the stone-flagged floor. At last he was done. He rubbed himself down with the rough towel. Dressed.

They did not meet his eye. The chaplain read continually from his book of prayers. The other bound his hands with a cord. A door was swung aside on cold air and the wash of first light over frosted earth. Then he saw it. It came at him like a scream. Thirteen steps. There would be thirteen steps. Blue skies. Limpid light. Men were crowded into the yard below. Joseph Carter! Weeping. He was clutching his smock frock, trying to cover his face with it. Cook's legs were shaking. He stumbled. A heavy arm steadied him. Father! Robert Wright was speaking but not to him. Early morning. A white cloth covered his eyes.

Whiteness. Snow. Thirteen steps. Purple moor grass. Hares wet with morning dew were leaping and loping out of the grass in the spacious lightness of a blue morning. Joseph Carter in tears! A hare leapt. A rush of movement. The sky was dead.

THE TIMES, 17th JANUARY 1831 EXECUTION OF HENRY COOK AT WINCHESTER (From a Correspondent)

*H*ENRY COOK, CONDEMNED *to death by the recent Special Commission held in this city for the vicious attack on Mr Bingham Barrents with a heavy sledgehammer, was executed this morning. The violence of the attack and his cruel and vindictive disposition as evinced in his attempt to strike Mr Barrents a second blow are sufficient justification for the government to select him as a suitable victim for the vengeance of the law. A story is afloat here respecting this man, which I think it right to mention, although I cannot trace it to any sufficient authority. It is said that he is guilty of forcing out with a skewer the eye of a favourite horse belonging to a former master who had offended him.*

The place of execution at Winchester is behind the gaol. The drop was erected on the front of its outer wall and the way to it is over a narrow gallery formed for the occasion on the top of two walls, which separate two of the felons' yards from each other. A number of the felons in the prison were turned out to witness the execution. The open space at the back of the prison is very narrow, but there was more than enough room for the spectators. From the situation in which I stood in the interior of the prison, I could not see any of the people on the outside, but I am told that they did not exceed two hundred and most of these were special constables who were ordered to attend. A barrier was erected on the outside of the prison, within which the special constables were ranged. They took their stations within it at half-past seven in the morning and remained there until the conclusion of the execution. A garret window, which was nearly opposite to, and on a level with the drop, was filled with three well-dressed gentlemen, who must have seen more of the execution than any other persons except for those who were officially obliged to attend it. Very few of the peasantry of the county were in attendance. I understand that the general feeling amongst the individuals assembled below the scaffold, who did not form a hundredth part of the numbers usually assembled on these occasions, was that the execution might have been dispensed with.

At ten minutes past eight o'clock, Cook was brought out with the rope around his neck and his arms pinioned. He was preceded by the chaplain of the gaol, Reverend Wright. At that moment the prison bell began to toll. Cook's chest heaved with emotion almost to bursting, and he staggered so painfully along that I expected to see him fall at any moment. I have heard that he slept during the early part of the night, but towards morning became so weak that it was expected that he would not have the strength to support himself to the drop.

The chaplain began to read the funeral service over the living man. I cast my eyes down into the felons' yard and saw many of the convicts weeping openly, some burying their faces in their smock frocks, others wringing their hands convulsively, and others leaning for support against the walls of the yard unable to cast their eyes upward. On turning my eyes again to the drop, I found the white nightcap pulled over the unfortunate criminal and the chaplain concluding the funeral service. Immediately afterwards, the executioner drew the bolt and the drop fell suddenly with a slight crash consigning the guilty man to a violent and ignominious death.

Thus ended this melancholy but necessary sacrifice to the

offended laws of the country. That the spirit of insubordination, though checked for the present, is alive and well in this county, is evident from two daring facts. The dead man was left hanging for an hour. When the executioner came to cut down the body, a shambling man, haggard and woebegone, detached himself from a small group of onlookers. Beneath his wild black beard, his face had a yellowness about it, a lividness that looked like nothing human. He shouted execrations at the hangman seldom heard even from such a crowd: 'Shame! Down with him! Bah, murderer, bah! Come on body snatcher! Take away the man you've killed!' Further, within an hour from the corpse being removed from the scaffold there was chalked in large characters on the wall beneath it: 'Murder for murder. Blood for blood.'

18

THE HORRORS OF the day and the quick burst of anger that had seized him when Henry Cook had been cut down had left him sick and exhausted. A slow torpor and heaviness almost overcame him. Turning his back on the empty gallows and the words he had chalked on the prison wall, he walked along the cobbles with a loping sidelong lurch. He stumbled and steadied himself against a wall coughing and wheezing. Doom-ridden, his eyes were ringed with pain. His head swam. His stomach clenched and he retched violently but brought nothing up but a little acid brown juice. He sat in the inky shadows for some time, his cheeks sunken in his furrowed face. Street pools were beginning to freeze over. Moisture was clinging to his ragged black beard. Pulling his filthy ragged coat around him, he staggered to his feet, nearly slipped and fell, but managed to follow the wall to the warmth of a low beer house.

'Summat for ye,' said a large woman placing a small glass within his reach. 'Ye seem so down. It will put a bit of heart back into ye.'

He met her eyes and found no cunning there. She moved her greasy plumpness towards the jagged uproar of drinkers nearly obscured by the thick reeking blue fug of tobacco smoke. A harsh corvine laugh broke out. A man with a scar-marked face stood up so abruptly that he sent the wooden stool he was sitting on flying in his indignation. He removed a clay pipe from his fire-flushed face and uttered a threat as menacing as broken glass to the assembly. He turned and left slamming the door with such force it was a wonder it didn't splinter its wooden frame.

It was of no concern to the man from East Stratton. He

sullenly drank off the fiery yellow liquid in a single gulp and gazed deeply into the fire. Flames licked and enfolded the dry wood. Hot sap from the logs popped and spat. Scarves of flame formed tiny caves of molten gold edged with blue heat, of beauty and dead white ash. He thought of Henry Cook. He remembered what he had told him that night at the White Swan. He recalled Henry's voice, the tight excitement it held. 'The wind blows the fire inwards, but a hay or wheat rick well put together, will resist combustion for a length of time if it begins on the outside, so the risk is small.' He sat for some time, his face in flame shadows, following his train of thought. The hearth snapped and blazed. His dark eyes were full of pain and fire.

Three hours before dawn found him in a purple-black field. The grass crusted with frost under a steel-bright moon. His breath came in loud rasping sobs as he looked back at the dark outline of the rick-yard belonging to Bingham Barrents. His breathing steadied and he became aware of the night's seamless silence. He had done his best to fire the rick from below, close to the stone straddles which supported it. But perhaps it had resisted his efforts. Smoke! A scroll of smoke lifted from a deep ruddy glow in the heart of the rick. Suddenly, a fountain of sparks shot into the clear, cold sky and fell in clusters on the sides of the crafted mound of hay. Within moments swift streams of heat leapt with fire and flickering radiance. Whether funeral pyre or beacon of hope he did not know. A quiet roar reached his ears. A bell-like bark sounded the alarm followed by muffled voices and shouts.

He turned his back on Mr Bingham Barrents. There was a glittering brightness in his eyes. His forehead was beaded with large drops of feverish moisture. He would walk. He would walk out into the darkness until he could walk no more.

19

'I MUSTN'T TALK and I mustn't run,' piped the little girl. 'You walk beside your sister and don't go looking behind, hear?' said Mrs Reed kindly. 'Hold the holly like this, so it doesn't hurt your hand. And when you get to the church I'll have your coat for you. I know it's cold.'

The little group fell silent. Mrs Reed looked pensively at pewter skies. To the east was a slow paling behind dark clouds and soon a welling of yellow and pink. A rare shaft of sunlight broke through only to fade into muffled grey. Henry Cook had been a frequent visitor to her well swept hearth. She at work with a pair of long-shanked scissors, calico or twill, a hank of thread. He before the fire, his dark hair glowing ruddily, quite at home with her family. At the door, before returning to the darkness and the solitude of his life, he would tug his black hat over his eyes and calmly produce a hare or a 'long-tailed 'un' as he would call a pheasant. 'Thieving acorns and beech-mast he was,' he would say with a meaningful smile.

'Here it comes now,' said her oldest son straightening. He was with a group of young men in white smock frocks.

Mrs Reed's face furrowed and creased into runnels of sadness at the sight of the open wagon drawn by a single horse creeping down the road from Winchester towards them. Behind it walked the working people of the parishes. Some, white-haired with grim countenances, marched stiffly, their eyes watering in the wind. Wives grieved for husbands recently taken from them: husbands who would now go to the ends of the Earth without them. Mothers, blind to the leaden winter skies, the patches of untrodden snow in sunless hollows beside the road, saw their own lost sons. They all trudged behind the plain elm coffin which lay in the middle of the simple vehicle. All walked in solemn silence. A trace of a smile appeared briefly on Mrs Reed's lips at the sight of so many people. The curate had given permission for the burial to take place within the churchyard but he would not preside over it. Her eyes suddenly glistened with tears. 'Henry Cook,' she said quietly, 'you will never be forgot in these parts. Never! You may depend upon it!'

The wagon drew to a halt beside the group and Mrs Reed organised the six little girls in white carrying their evergreens to lead the melancholy procession and behind them the six young men in white smock frocks. They moved on to the freshly up-turned earth in the churchyard at Micheldever nearly a mile away. There, other mourners were waiting. Eight labourers lowered the coffin into the grave. A shovel lay across a pile of dirt to one side. Henry Cook's death cell was sealed and left to endure the slow siege of time.

Ann Mason's grey eyes widened in surprise. Farmer Deacle was in earnest conversation with the blacksmith from Sutton Scotney. They stood amongst gravestones sheltered from the wind by a high beech hedge. They joined her by the lych-gate.

'A sad day for the valley,' said Deacle plaintively.

'I, I thought you were...' stammered Ann confused. She nodded a greeting to the blacksmith.

Deacle noticed her grief-weary face, the webs about her eyes.

'I am a free man, pending a court hearing. Cobbett himself has taken an interest in the case. He assures me that there is a good chance of indicting Mr Bingham Barrents for wrongful arrest and assault. It is but a small justice,' he continued with a gleam of truculence in his eye. 'A rich man will pay a fine, Henry paid with his life.'

They lapsed into a sad silence.

'And Mrs Deacle?'

'She improves daily.' He looked at her intently. 'Ann, I know of your troubles. You will not want for meal and butter or an egg or two while the farm is mine. And there is work a plenty if you need it.'

'Aye!' added the blacksmith. 'And there's still many a good soul in Sutton to be sure. There will be coals from my own forge for ye too!'

Moisture filmed her eyes. She averted her face, struggled to control the surge of emotion. She would thank them, but not now. She gazed abstractedly at the gravestones standing like black teeth in the wet earth.

'Have you seen Joseph? Is he still in Winchester?' she asked tremulously, uncertain. 'With Eliza I have been unable to…' She shook with grief unable to continue.

'No,' said the big man tenderly, 'but the prison was so crowded that the silence broke down. I have heard men are being moved every few days to Portsmouth. It is done quietly and very early in the morning.'

The words struck her like an arrow. Thorn cruel. She looked at him entirely without hope.

'Then he could be gone already! I may never see him again!'

20

THE COLD, SURGING skies were zinc-grey. The street was in winter shadow and the night's frost unmelted making the cobblestones treacherous. The high prison walls had a skirting of snow. Ann pleaded softly in silent prayer that Joe might still be behind those oozing walls of dark brick and stone. She pulled her shawl more tightly around herself and quickened her step. Three times since Henry Cook's funeral she had walked the seven miles into Winchester in the hope of catching a glimpse of her husband. But this morning something was happening. Her heart jumped in sudden hope. There was a small crowd of ragged women gathered outside the prison gates. Raw-cheeked, hair awry, their faces were grim, grey, hard-lined from savage want and grief. They spoke quietly, their voices little more than a toneless mutter. Ann stood with them in the bleak light, withdrawn and solemn.

In the prison courtyard was a great bay horse. Blinkered and in heavy harness, it stood in front of a covered cart with one foot raised. A woman near Ann suddenly gave out a loud strangulated cry, a shrill wailing sound and the throng surged forward pressing themselves against the iron of the gates, calling and shouting discordantly. A line of eight men walked awkwardly towards the wagon. Ann searched frantically amidst the turmoil for Joe. For an instant she did not recognise the figure shambling along with a strange uneven gait as her husband. He was in irons! His feet were heavy and chained! He was about to climb up into the wagon. It was cruel to see the face she loved so full of pain.

'Joe! Joe! It's Ann! I'm here!' But her voice was lost in the short, wild confusion of sound and trampling, pressing bodies.

Joe thought he heard his name. He paused and hurriedly searched the faces of the women. His chest tightened and he laboured in his breathing, but he did not see Ann. He was pushed roughly into the dimness of the cart. The doors of the wagon were made secure. Gaolers opened the gates and forced the women aside. The big horse strained against its load, its white-starred forehead nodded as the heavy wood and iron wheels began to turn. Its hooves clopped on the cobblestones. A woman, her matted black hair streaming down her back like wet seaweed over her shabby coat, stumbled madly after the cart for a little distance crying in wild distress. Her face was twisted with anguish as she shouted. She fell heavily into the street. She sat there, a stooped and shapeless form, like a thing abandoned. Her nose leaked blood. Her lips were already purpling into a pulpy plum red.

Disconsolate, Ann stood still and rigid against the wet prison wall. She pressed her clenched fists against her face. Her eyes mute and yearning followed the cart. She began to cry quietly. The chaos in her left her weak and unable to think. He was gone. Gone!

21

Yes, it irritated him. It irked him increasingly. He pursed his lips and unfolded the thick sheets of paper for the third time that morning.

To you Sir this comes with greetings,

I take the liberty of addressing a few lines to you knowing that letters of this sort are not pleasant. It is my luck; some would say misfortune, to be confined within the walls of a gaol. I am here on your account and as this is a private letter, I want to ask you a few questions concerning the matter. Let us reason together for it seems to me some things are wrong and need to be set right.

At the late assizes you were my prosecutor, and the charge was 'robbing' you of five shillings. Now, it would take much time and strong argument to persuade me that your arguments for punishing me were motivated by a sense of justice, and it would take a head more solid than Mr Baron Vaughan's to convince me that I ever gained a sixpence in a dishonest way. I do not know whether he can say the same of himself. Five shillings could not have been a great loss to you – there was not the least injury done or threatened to your person and you were thanked for your donation. Why then did you charge me with robbery and do your best to send me to the gallows? If not justice it must be ill-will towards me.

How have I offended? I who so rarely spoke to you? There can be only one way and that is my political opinions differ from your own. 'Many men, many minds' is the common saying amongst us. But as to the present, people are of one mind, there is great need for change. How many times have you addressed me in the language

of the church as a 'dearly beloved brother'? How often have I heard
you pray for 'the prisoner and the captive'; for 'fatherless children
and widows and all that are desolate and oppressed'? God says in
Deuteronomy 'Cursed is he that smiteth his brother secretly'. You
have not followed the word of him who cannot err!

If your injury were directed solely at me I would not care. I have
been blessed with a healthy body and sound mind, but you deprive
my mother of the last means of support by taking me from her, for
you cannot be in ignorance of the fate of my brother Joseph. At the
age of nearly seventy, she has seen her sons torn from her side and
treated like thieves and vagabonds. Sir, you have not forgiven your
brother 'seventy times seven' as was Christ's advice to Peter.

Yours dutifully,
Robert Mason

P.S. Since writing the above, I have spoken with Enos Diddams
and he told me that you prosecuted me because Thomas Barrents
in a manner compelled you. Wait on Sir Thomas and show him
this letter. It will suit him for he is a very religious man. Tell him
I wish him such a conscience as Judas had after betraying the
Saviour of Men!

The Reverend James Joliffe flung the thing from him. The
effrontery of the man! Let him wither into age in some distant
land. He didn't care! Nevertheless, anxiety gnawed at him.
Earlier in the morning he had read with genuine feeling to the
few women who now constituted his diminished congregation,
the prayer the Privy Council had ordered from the Archbishop
on account of the troubled state of certain parts of England.
It, too, lay on his desk. He picked it up and the ink stain which
always filled him with a troubling disgust leapt at him. There
it stubbornly remained like a darkened soul in spite of Mrs
Ashby's continued efforts to remove it. His eyes flicked over
part of the Archbishop's missive.

Restore, O Lord, to Thy people the quiet enjoyment of the many and great blessings which we have received from Thy bounty: defeat and frustrate the malice of wicked and turbulent men, and turn their hearts: have pity, O Lord, on the simple and ignorant, who have been led astray, and recall them to a sense of their duty...

He had, he thought, quite cleverly added to the Archbishop's prayer an old fable, which he considered to be a powerful parable of the present times.

A herd of swine, prowling about on an autumnal day, assembled under a fine oak, whose branches were loaded with acorns; not satisfied with the share scattered on the green sward, eager to secure the whole, they burrowed beneath the root till the tree fell, and trampling amidst the broken boughs with brutal greediness, devoured the fruit, heeding not that it was the last produce they could ever hope to derive from a tree, under whose shade the flocks of the forest had fed, and the shepherds who guarded them had reposed from generation to generation.

The faces below the pulpit had remained morose and silent. 'Bah!' he said aloud in exasperated contempt, 'I may as well preach to a flock of goslings!'

His bitter reverie was disturbed by a clatter of hooves and voices below his window. His heart gave a momentary anxious lurch. He moved to the window in time to see a man with lank red hair in high riding boots wheeling a black gelding away from Mrs Ashby. His curiosity would soon be satisfied. Mrs Ashby, pigeon-plump, was doing her best to hurry towards his door.

'It was Mr Callendar from Stratton Park with a letter from Sir Thomas!' she said breathlessly.

'Thank you, Mrs Ashby, that will be all,' he said, trying to keep the rising emotion out of his voice.

It was an invitation to dine at Stratton Park! He felt a shadow lift from him, a great flowering of relief. He closed his eyes for a moment. Breathed deeply. It was as if he had already been driven through the stone gateposts guarded by weathered lions and unicorns; had already walked the chessboard marble entrance hall and taken his seat at the long table amongst the glitter of glass and china. Outside in the garden peacocks would give their strident cries in the clear wintry dusk.

He stood and dropped the invitation onto the desk. It neatly hid the unsightly ink stain and called, 'Mrs Ashby! Mrs Ashby!'

22

THERE WERE THREE heavy stamps on the deck above his head.

'Far-polens so-ho! Twelve o'clock there below hear the news!'

Sailors! Damn them! Couldn't they move a pound weight or pull a rope without hollering? Between decks the close stench of acrid sweat and damp wool which hung in the cramped sleeping quarters of the prison caught in his throat. He gave a stifled hoarse cough, trying not to disturb Robert and the other men sleeping so close to him. He could feel sweat on the sides of his body and on his neck and forehead. There in the darkness he was aware of the pulse and wash of the sea; the creak and roll of the ship. At least he had been spared the misery of sea-sickness. After leaving Portsmouth, he and Robert had seen the last of the hills of Cornwall sink below the horizon under a trumpet-flared sunset. When the ship began its long roll up and down the swell and collapse of waves, the movement had unsettled Robert. His face paled and his shoulders hunched and tightened. He opened his mouth wide and took great gulps of wet air in an attempt to quell the unease but his stomach convulsed and he was violently ill. He had grown more accustomed to the rhythm of the ship but he still occasionally heaved in bouts of blinding nausea that gave him little relief.

A chill and empty melancholy gripped Joseph. He could not go back! A widening ocean lay between him and England. The anguish of separation had come as unexpectedly and as unbidden as a fatal disease – unthought-of, but inexorable and unrelenting. It was as irreversible as death. Such was the chance nature of human undertakings. He carried the pain within him constantly. He willingly consented to it. A school of dolphins arcing from silver water or the flight of wind-blown gulls plunging in broken circles only nourished the pain. He would close his eyes and pursue with all his strength images of those he loved. He was severed, not only from Ann and little Eliza, but also from his home as well. His lost land so neatly contained in its hedgerows and freestone walls. To forget was to betray but memory was demanding and fallible. It filled him with remorse and savage guilt when he could not imagine small characteristic gestures of Ann or precise details of her face. He was a man who relished moments of solitude but now in the crowded quarters of the ship he was lonely. It was a loneliness that was uncomplicated and absolute. A bell was struck by the duty watch above. He thought of the wooden ship as if from a great distance caught in the immensities of sea and night sky. He felt a tiredness in his eyes and he closed them. Weariness spread through his body. He slept.

The air began filling with light. Those convicts who had been selected as cooks were the first to be admitted to the decks. At sunrise the prison doors were thrown open for all. The bathing tub was placed in position on deck and soon, amidst laughter, buckets of water were poured gleefully over each other in the blue-bright windy morning under a sun that was already too bright. Joseph smiled wryly as he threw water at Robert's bare torso. All the convicts on board the *Eleanor* were 'Swing Men' like himself. There was little to fear from them. The day ahead was predictable enough. At six o'clock rations were served out to the mess men, and while they were below, volunteers swabbed the deck. All bedding was then brought up and secured on deck with two pieces of sennit. At eight, breakfast was served and afterwards the prison deck was dry-holystoned. He and Robert then conducted school for those who wanted to improve their reading and writing. Those not attending picked oakum or worked at their trades. Sherbet, a mixture of lime juice and sugar, was served before the noon meal. The wine allowance was given after the meal under the watchful eye of Stephenson, the surgeon, to prevent any trafficking. Schools met again in the afternoon, supper was served at four o'clock followed by games and singing on deck. At sunset all were mustered and the prison locked. The routine was varied only by wet or squally weather, or by the workings of the ship.

There was a shout from above. Mason looked up. The straining white sails were like the wings of some gigantic bird. A sailor swaying in the rigging was pointing to starboard. His voice lost in the wind. The first mate, his lean brown face split into a smile at the antics with the buckets, turned and gobbed over the gunwale. He too began to shout.

'Fish! Flying fish!'

Joseph and the others moved towards the first mate. His sunburnt eyes were alive with excitement.

'Look!' he exclaimed, pointing to the crested billows of the waves.

Joseph clenched his watering eyes shut against the sea-dazzle. Opened them again to the wavering brightness. A swarm of dark, grey-blue fish perhaps fifteen inches long burst powerfully out of the mounds of rolling water and glided on wing-like fins. There were more! Lunging from the glittering sea in a frenzied panic, leaping, splashing, flying. Flicking their veined-glass fins insect-like, they remained airborne for perhaps fifty yards before plummeting to the dangers they were fleeing below the water.

'Carry on there, sir, if you please,' came a salty voice. The ship's master looking down on them from the quarterdeck breathed out smoke with the words from a short brown pipe. It was said firmly. It was meant to be heard.

'Right you are, sir,' said the first mate. He straightened his spare frame and gave instructions for the clearing of tub and buckets from the deck.

Hyde Park Barracks,
Sydney
Wednesday 13th July, 1831

My dear Ann, Mother and Eliza,

This comes with my love to you all hoping by the blessing of Providence it may find you all in good health, a privilege I myself enjoy. My spirits though are much depressed as I miss you all sorely. My dear Ann I will give you an account of my life and travels since I was taken from you so roughly – already so long ago!

We were taken from Winchester early in the morning in a closed prison van in irons and chained together. Yes, your husband in leg irons! Bazzels and chains they call them. Ten days later we were at sea. I have seen but little of the world and was at first deeply afraid. The sea leapt and seethed and when the wind was 'dead aft' as the sailors call it the ship rolled from side to side. Poor Robert suffered greatly from sickness. You cannot see as far on the water as you might think and when the sea was rough a wave would rise like a great hill before us. The ship would climb to the shoulder of the swell and then dive into the trough while the wave fled under our stern. There was beauty too. When the wind was brisk and combed the crests of waves into wisps of spray that jetted up over our bow there were constant rainbows in the sunshine. The water was a deep beautiful green paling to blue as we sailed further and further south. At night as the ship dashed through the waves the water sparkled and appeared full of stars, like a cat's coat when you rub it in the dark.

Our captain talked of putting into Rio de Janeiro for fresh water but we fell in with another trade wind which carried us to the Cape of Good Hope. We cast anchor in Simon's Bay on the 27th of April. We were not permitted to go ashore but we were anchored close enough to read the names over the shop doors. The town appeared to be very neat and clean and it lies at the foot of a soaring range of barren mountains. The rocks at its summit appear ready to tumble down at any moment to crush the white houses with their green shutters. It is now an English settlement but the people displayed every shade from jet black to fair English lady. We stayed ten days and every morning we were startled by the report of a gun from a man-of-war in the harbour. The sound bounced and echoed striking against the sides of rocks and recoiling into the deep narrow chasms and ravines of the range until it died in muffled silence.

From want of wind the ship was still in sight of land a day after leaving, nor did we gain much distance in the next three days. The sea was sluggish and the sails drooped lifelessly. But there followed days of storm and crying wind. Waves came over the bulwarks and put out the fire every time an attempt was made to light one. We could get no food cooked and lived on dry biscuit for three days. At the end of May we sailed between two islands named Amsterdam and St Paul also known as the Islands of Desolation. They were little more than bare rugged hilltops jutting up out of a lonely sea. We saw no more land until we entered Bass Strait which separates Van Diemen's Land and New South Wales. The sea swell was dreadful with deep and awful gulfs. It was here that we suddenly lost the great white birds which had followed us in large numbers all the way from Africa. One sailor informed me that they were the souls of drowned seamen, another that the albatross is a sign of good luck, yet another that it signalled bad luck! Whatever superstitions they vested in them it did not stop some cruel sailors from trying to catch one by throwing a strong hook baited with a piece of beef or pork into the sea and letting it drag in the foaming wake of the vessel.

We dropped anchor in Sydney Cove on the 25th of June

completing our journey in eighteen weeks. The sailors declared it the finest voyage they had known. The town of Sydney stands by the side of a hill. The houses are mainly of stone and look out onto a blue bay surrounded by rising ground covered with trees and shrubs. We remained on board until the 11th of July when we were permitted to come on shore in our own clothes. This was considered quite an unusual indulgence by the people. It seems that to be an honest man is a valuable qualification here! We are to remain at the barracks until we are claimed by our masters and have been given firm instructions not to have any correspondence with those sent here for crimes. This relieved me greatly. The Governor has assigned masters to us all and we wait in great suspense to know our destiny. Although it is several months since I left you and my native land it will be a sad parting from Robert and my shipmates who have come from parts of England not remote from Bullington. They are for the most part men of honest principle. My future with you has been stolen from me. I await what is to replace the theft in fearful anxiety. When I leave these barracks I will walk out into the unknown.

My dear Ann, I am 15,000 miles from home! Tell Enos Diddams that if there should be a reformed Parliament, I hope that the people of Sutton, Barton and Bullington will be the first, who will present a petition for the return of those convicted at the Special Assizes. William Cobbett will be in that Parliament and he is a compassionate man. If this does not happen it may be possible for you to join me. I have heard there is an office in London where if women apply they are sent out to their husbands and with a special licence it may be possible to have me assigned to you. You would be my master! But we cannot puzzle our brains with but half a story! Robert says to tell the people of Bullington he is unchanged, that he is Robert Mason still! I will forward the address of my whereabouts as soon as I know myself. Tell me if

you are at Bullington. Tell me about Eliza. Tell me all the news
you can in every description.

I remain
Yours
Joseph Mason

23

'MASON! JOE MASON!'

The call had come, as he knew it must. There followed moments of confused emotions, confused and inadequate farewells as he gathered up his few belongings and walked towards the prison officer and a man beside him dressed in fustian, his face a wrinkled brown under clean grey hair. It was a morning of cloudless blue sky and blustering wind which lifted the dust and blurred the sounds of fife and drum from the nearby exercise yard.

They had passed through the main barrack gate and had left the long line of barrack-wall behind them before the man paused on the narrow rain-torn path. A tightening of his lips passed for a smile; a cursory nod for an introduction.

'Lane. Ross Lane, I'm Macarthur's man.' He raised a corner of his mouth in wry amusement. 'And as if you haven't done enough sailin' we are for the King's Wharf and Parramatta.'

They came to an open marketplace surrounded by the remains of an old three-rail fence. Settlers' drays spread with local vegetables, bundles of green grass and sacks of maize stood amongst shed-like stalls of dealers. Here Sydney was alive in the cool air. Livestock bellowed. A man burdened with a bunch of squawking hens slung over his shoulders swore viciously at dirt-grained children chasing a fugitive fowl which ran screeching through the manure and dust. Street sellers pushing barrow carts called out prices in a litany praising the few goods they had for sale. A fire in the centre of the square gave off a stink of burnt rags. Lean dogs barked or slept in the lemon light of the dusty sun. Turning into George Street Mason posted his letter to Ann at the Post Office. He was not certain that she was still at Bullington. She may have gone into service or found work on a distant farm. Nor did he know if his mother were still alive. He prayed silently that it would reach them. It cost eight pence leaving him with sixpence. He and Robert had left England with two sovereigns each but had been persuaded to give them up to the ship's doctor for safe keeping only to learn in Sydney that the money had been placed in a savings bank and there it would remain until they were free.

The lack of close restraint seemed strange to Mason. Not only was he free to openly post his letter but his convict garb was the same as ordinary working people. He in no way stood out from the crowds around him. The barracks had buzzed with talk of the new governor, Richard Bourke, who was publically opposed to transportation and believed that the system would soon come to an end. It was a measure of his approach that his enemies in the colony who were opposed to his liberal sentiments dubbed him the 'convicts' friend'. Prisoners under sentence were no longer to wear irons unless by special order. They could now marry and their children would be free. It seemed that a man's occupation, what he could do was all important, not his past. It was according to this principle that he had been assigned to a master of whom he knew nothing. His fate rested with him.

The road narrowed and began to climb the side of a ridge and follow the twists and turns of random layers of sandstone which fell like steps to the western shore of the cove. Half-hidden makeshift hovels in narrow alleys clung haphazardly to the uneven ground and Mason was suddenly assaulted by the stark stench of rotting vegetation and clotted, filthy ditches. A rat bunched in a squirm of excitement and disappeared up a dripping water pipe dragging its naked tail in behind it. A woman leaned in a doorway and searched Mason's face with a look of rouged voluptuous melancholy.

Sick at heart, Mason eyed his taciturn companion dubiously and tried to engage him in conversation.

'What sort of man can I expect my master to be?' he asked tentatively.

Lane stopped walking. He stood stolidly for a moment, fingering his upper lip with a forefinger then parried the question with a phlegmy cough before answering.

'When he was younger and a magistrate, I've heard that he sentenced a man such as yerself, a servant of the governor, to a flogging of twenty-five lashes every morning until he confessed where goods that he had stole were hid. That's our man is Mr Macarthur.'

It was Mason's turn to be silent. He had heard tales from sailors very different from those he had heard at the barracks. Of men tied with leather thongs, the leaping red hell of the lash and the white flame of salt.

'But my advice is this,' Lane continued having noted the effect of his speech on Mason. 'What masters want is willing workers. All a man has got to mind is to keep his tongue in his head and do his master's bidding, and then he is looked upon the same as if he were at home back in the old country.' The solemnity of his face was lost in a smile. 'The floggings happened a long time ago. Even if the man were still a magistrate it takes a court order to have a man flogged nowadays. Things have changed. In many ways you will live as a free man. The land itself is your prison and it doesn't exactly flow with milk and honey.'

Voices and laughter spilled out into the street from the straw and the sopped tables of a squalid public house. Saturday afternoon.

'We won't be able to sail until this evening with this wind. I'll leave you here for the time being and collect you later. There's nought you can do for the boatmen.'

In a moment he was gone.

Mason stood awkwardly in the doorway of the tap-room, glimpsed a leering, long-jowled face full of sly wickedness and caught the sharp hot stink of reeking rum. He could not face it. Trembling with fear and nerves he turned to the street instead. But hunger gnawed at him as he paced aimlessly to and fro along the slippery cobbles which oozed dampness. He had had nothing to eat before leaving the barracks that morning and the bread that he and Robert had bought there was so bad they could not eat it. He had not tasted beer since he left England. The thought of the acid-sharp tang of it cheered him a little. He had sixpence. He squared his shoulders and entered the house in search of its ale if not its company.

It was almost suffocatingly full. Men were divided into groups of twos, threes and fours. And there was hardly an individual who did not have the darkened stump of a filthy pipe jammed between his teeth. Some wore straw hats, some beavers, some caps of untanned kangaroo skin. Some wore neck-handkerchiefs, some none. The place buzzed and murmured, slashed through by the dominating voice of a fat bristly fellow who sat at a wooden bench with the heel of a loaf of bread and a wine glass full of rum in front of him.

'Breeding counts yer know!' he said loudly in a slurred drunken voice to a woman mopping the table with a dirty rag.

She said nothing. Morose and stubborn and drunk herself she reeled away from the man and his ribaldries. A pale waif of a girl, perhaps eleven years old, was at her side waiting for commands or blows. Her long hair was lank like old string. Her feet were bare.

A small pewter mug of ale slid towards Mason and he placed his last coin into a large dimpled hand.

'What's this now?' said the publican, eyeing the silver. 'That's no good to me. You would do better in India with that.'

Mason flared in shame at the discovery of the tawdry deception he had unwittingly committed. The coin that he had taken for a sixpence was from some foreign country and of no value in the colony. He started to stand but the large hand of the publican forced him down. His eyes began to laugh.

'Have yer beer, man. On the house – such as it may be. Yer welcomed to it.'

Mason, writhing inwardly, muttered embarrassed thanks.

Cheek in his cupped hand, the fat man was leering at the charwoman as she bent over a fireless hearth. His small red-streaked eyes had a sharp gleam of cruel enjoyment in them. The child squatted beside her sweeping dead ashes into a flat pan. The man's stout blackthorn stick which had been leaning against the table fell with a clatter to the floor. Perhaps he had nudged it over with his boot.

'Pick it up!' he demanded sourly.

'Pick it up yerself and be buggered!' the woman burst out viciously. She pulled up her sleeves as if she were prepared to fight him there and then. 'Yer no match for me!'

The man stood up so violently that he knocked his chair over.

'Shut ya gob, damn ya!' the man bellowed, lunging towards her, his chest heaving and his eyes awash with sudden anger.

He caught the woman a heavy smack on the side of her head just as the child brought his own walking stick down across his temple. He fell heavily onto the already overturned chair which cracked under his weight. The child shrieked like a parakeet, staggered backwards flinging the stick away from her.

'Bugger your eyes! What have you done to me?' He put both his hands against his forehead for a moment. His face the colour of suet streamed with blood. 'You dunghill! You'll look like pigs' chitterlings when I'm finished with you, ya mutt!' he almost sobbed, struggling to his feet.

'Get out!' roared the publican, shoving him with all the strength of his right arm through the doorway. Bending down he retrieved the ugly black stick from the boarded floor and threw it after the man now sprawled on the dung-coated cobbles. He managed to get to his feet and remained there swaying precariously. His temple swollen and purpling, he rained vile curses on the world. Exhausting himself, he at last fell silent, threw back his heavy shaggy head and moved it from side to side as if to give some relief to his thick neck. He shook himself; shivered, beast-like; shuddered; and heeling over sideways in his drunkenness and filth disappeared down a slit of an alley in the labyrinth of grimy streets.

The publican stood like a wrestler in his apron, his arms folded. He turned to the woman.

'Get back to your work!'

She quietened into sullen silence. Her dingy face looked stale and drawn. She stood dully in front of her employer, looking vulnerable despite her work-roughened features and plump strong arms. She began to cry, sniffing rapidly. Her daughter buried her face in her skirts.

'Here, take this,' Mason said, beckoning the girl to him. He held the small useless coin out to her. Her dirty hand closed over it in an instant.

Shocked to numbness at the violence, he then closed his eyes and massaged his brow with thumb and middle finger trying to calm his jolted nerves. He remembered the many pleasant nights he had spent in front of the ruddy hearth of the Swan, the walk home after singing and conversation, the purple-black fields, the air clover fresh beside the stream. It had seemed nothing at the time, something almost unnoticed, but now he recalled it with such nostalgia that it caused him physical pain.

There was a shambling crash at the door and for a moment Joseph feared the man had returned, but instead he saw the compact wiry figure of the first mate of the *Eleanor*. The man's eyes snagged on Mason sitting at his wooden bench along the wall and he greeted him with a bright, direct, quizzical expression.

'What! Joe Mason! How is it that I find you in such a place as this?'

Joseph, his face still taut with apprehension and disgust explained as well as he could.

'Have you any money?'

Mason glanced at the girl who had resumed her work at the cold hearth.

'Not a penny,' he said with a vague hopeless gesture of his hands. He looked candidly into the sandy-lashed eyes of the mate and felt himself sag with relief and gratitude at the presence of the man.

'Simmons!' the mate called to the master of the house, 'bread, cheese and ale for an old shipmate of mine.'

'But – but I can't…' stammered Mason.

The mate laughed noiselessly, slapped a shilling for him onto the table, and wished him the best of luck.

A copper sun nudged the horizon then plunged rapidly leaving a cloudless afterglow. The wind had become favourable and the small vessel glided effortlessly up the river. Mason, sprawled in the stern, looked up at high barren banks and low rocky cliffs which the river had gnawed into caves and crannies and inlets. Beyond them loomed tall untidy trees in the inky shadows of the short dusk. There was something deeply ancient about the place in a way he could feel but not articulate. With the darkness came a steel-bright moon and sharp brilliant stars. The air had a limpid coolness and beads of dew formed on the railings and glinted grey on the decking. He sank into a shallow drowse and thought of Ann. He could see her sitting on the doorstep in the sun shelling a trug of peas; walking beside a willow-strewn stream; hanging out boiled bed sheets white in a blue sky-washed morning. A sudden depression blanketed him. They would grow old apart. The separation would last forever. They could not even look up at the same night sky or share the same season on the Earth. There was only the past. Bullington was marooned in the past.

The boat shuddered to a halt. The men had deviated from the deep channel and the bow had lifted itself up onto a shoal of pebbled sand. It occupied the boatmen for some time. Their voices frayed with irritation and became direct and uncouth before their skills or the tide released the vessel. Then they were for visiting what they called the half-way house, little more than a bark hovel some distance from the river, where they remained for an hour before returning with satisfied smacks of the lips and bursts of easy laughter. When at last they arrived at a landing on Macarthur's reach it was decided that it was far too late to disturb the household and that it would be best if Lane and Mason spent what was left of the night in Parramatta with one of the boatmen. Later Mason had only a vague recollection of sheds and rusted metal in disarray, a dark room and of breathing in the smothering odours of cooking and dust and chicken dirt before subsiding in quick exhaustion into a dreamless sleep.

He woke in the grey of the morning to the clatter of ladle and pot made by a large fleshy woman who greeted him with no more than a sidelong glance. Her clothes gave out a thick stale stink of wood smoke. Her hair fell uncombed and matted to her shoulders. Flies buzzed in the room which reeked of raw liquor and years of impotent rage. A large white parrot with a sun-yellow crest slumped silently in a cage where it morosely plucked at its feathers leaving patches of its wrinkled blue-grey skin exposed. The boatman was already about in his flannel shirt. They made a hasty breakfast of some boiled salted beef before escaping the woman's tortured scowling expression and unnatural silence into the wide streets of Parramatta. There they parted company. The boatman set off towards the river leaving Mason and Lane to walk the two miles to Vineyard Cottage.

Mason half-closed his eyes against the glare, the first flames of the day. They walked some distance along a raised footpath with the road on one side and paling fences in varying states of repair on the other. Other than the church and a row or two of stone houses, most of the scattered dwellings were of weatherboard and shingle, not a few were built of slab and covered with bark giving the town a ragged, makeshift appearance. The shadeless street was empty save for a large brindle dog which slouched across the road. Mason jumped at the sudden sharp discharge from a heavy unseen rifle which struck the stray dog in its hindquarters sending it rolling and howling into a roadside ditch. There it flailed its paws violently until it was shaken by long shudders into stillness.

Unnerved, Mason stood bolt upright in confused alarm in the tense thickening silence.

'More dogs than men in this country,' said Lane drily. 'There must be twenty of the mongrels roaming Macarthur's place. The local constables receive a small payment for killing any dog without a collar with its owner's name on it.' He twisted his lip sardonically and smiled wanly at Mason's distress. 'Alas for the local population it is not stipulated who is to remove the rotting remains.'

Mason blinked nervously in the quivering light. His face was drawn. He felt old. A crow alighted on the yellow grass that grew beside the ditch and hopped triumphantly towards the dog. Mason hoped it was dead and not still dying.

A flock of parrots, spring green, exploded out of a tree massed with yellow flowers and streaked away dipping sharply across a small open field. Mr Hannibal Macarthur stood solidly with his legs slightly apart on the steps of his substantial stone house and waited for the men to approach. Beyond the house a thin plume of cloud melted into soft blues and violet distance.

He nodded to Lane.

'Joseph Mason,' he said neutrally and extended his hand briefly.

Mason was surprised at the dry rough hardness of it.

'Lane will show you around,' he said measuredly, flicking a shred of tobacco from his mouth with a finger.

Mason guessed him to be about forty, perhaps a little older. His face was hard, blunt and unsophisticated. The metallic purity of his eyes allowed no levity. Laughter would be uncommon in this place. It was easy to believe Lane's story that he had once flogged a confession out of a man.

Vineyard Cottage,
nr Parramatta
26th September, 1831

My Dear Ann, Mother and Eliza,
I pray that this letter may find you at Bullington and that you are all safe and well. I live in constant hope of seeing you again one day. I can get no newspaper at all but I go to Parramatta every Sunday to the Methodist chapel and I hear a little news sometimes. There is some sympathy for us here and rumours that we will be emancipated in six months. If this is true I would advise you not to come for I would return to England if I had my liberty and not stay in this country. I am sorry to say that among the community at large it is a rare thing to find someone, man or woman, who does not drink to excess, quarrel, fight and use the vilest language that tongue can utter.

I have had word from Robert who seems in good spirits. He has been assigned to Major Benjamin Sullivan who is a magistrate at Port Macquarie, but the property where he will work is on the Hunter River upstream from Newcastle. How he learned of my whereabouts is a complete mystery to me, but happy I was to pay the four pence for his letter!

I have no reason to complain. I receive good treatment and I have plenty of bread and beef. I live in a hut near the garden where I work with a man from Upton. His name is Alderman but here he goes by the name of Armats. Does mother know of the family? It is some consolation to talk to him of places familiar to us both but it is also a sad reminder of happier days in Hampshire! We have to cook our own meals and wash our own clothes, but it is better to have to cook one's own victuals than have none to cook. I have become quite a dab hand at baking a kind of bread common here. Firstly, I put flour on a clean sheet of bark I keep for the purpose, and then I shake a little salt onto it and wet it up with water. After kneading it and pressing it flat I find a clean place for it in the hearth and bury it in hot ashes until ready. I beat the ashes off with a green switch and have become quite accustomed to its taste!

The hut is made from slabs split out of trees and set upright. The roof is made up of strips of bark tied to the rafters with green hide. The floor is trampled earth. A rough bed, a rude table and fireplace complete the furnishings. Many cowsheds and pigsties in England are palaces compared with such a dwelling. The garden is about four acres but most of it has never seen a hoe. We have put some cabbages and potatoes into it but there has not been enough rain to lay the dust. There has been little cold. In June and July the nights were frosty but it is a rare thing to see ice as thick as a shilling here. Where I am is surrounded by woods. I have been told that there are large dangerous snakes but fortunately I have not yet seen one. The trees are very large and high and do not drop their leaves in winter, although there are some called gum trees which shed their bark making them look strangely naked. What is cleared are little more than dots. It would take the labour of thousands, nay, I might say millions of people ages to fell such forests.

I have lived here at Vineyard Cottage for ten weeks and have learned its sounds and smells, its routines and its work, but tomorrow I am to leave for Westwood, another of Macarthur's farms, which is some thirty miles away and closer to what are called the Blue Mountains.

A bitter melancholy settles upon me. I write this through swimming eyes. I miss you with the purest feeling of loss. I long to feel the weight of Eliza's head on my shoulder; I long to hold you in my arms, but I am cut off from everyone – from the world as a whole. I will carry to the grave the injustice served upon me and will never understand why I should be banished from my native country for advocating the cause of those who *lived in a land of plenty, yet never knew what it was to have enough.*

Write to me care of Mr Hannibal Macarthur of Vineyard Cottage near Parramatta.

I remain
Yours
Joseph Mason

24

EVERYTHING HUMMED, SHRILLED, buzzed, clicked – the rasping sounds seemed to emanate from the air itself – or the sticky yellow heat. Summer. The tedium of it settled upon him like a grey mildew. The back of his shirt was wet; tiny bush flies adhered themselves to the dampness, searched his eyes for moisture. His arms burned and peeled as he tended the green profusion of bean and pumpkin vines. Then taking up a hoe he worked between the rows of Indian corn, hilling the stalks as he went. He was pleased with his garden. It now produced melons as large as a four gallon water bucket. A year ago it was a barren acre overrun with weeds and as hard as a turnpike road. He had had to carry water to the few struggling cabbage stalks from the nearby stream and then that had dried into a torment of rock and cracked dry clay. And always there had been the smell of burning in the wind. They were clearing the forests. A pageant of fire lit the night with ruddy brilliance as flames leaped to reach a cluster of trees as yet untouched leaving behind a desolate landscape as black as ink, obscure and silent, with perhaps a single trunk, hollow, headless, chimney-like poised above the ashes.

This, his second January, had brought storms of rain sweeping across from the mountains to drum on roofs and claw at window panes. White mushrooms appeared in washed sunlight in parts of the paddocks. Withered grass flourished. But now the sun was bright, pitiless, probing. The air was hot and still, attracting small flying insects. He straightened his back. A great eagle swam through the clear mass of sky, swung in the hard light, stepping higher on the blue spiral of warm air. In the distance the mountains were shrouded with haze. He was imprisoned in scrub, timber and silence, in a land endlessly alien and indifferent to him. His sun-prison shimmered between pale sky and distance. Little by little he was learning to abandon himself to the silence and the loneliness. Choices, he now knew, were not an act of free will. They were prescribed, compelled, ingrained in circumstance and personality.

The trees were holding the last of the light when he made his way towards the small building called the kitchen which was detached from the main cottage and where he slept and had his meals with a free man and his wife. A privilege granted by Macarthur, but he waited in line with the other assigned men to have his rations weighed out, always refusing the tobacco for which he had no use. Taking off his shirt he washed outside in a tin basin feeling the first of the evening breeze cool on his skin. The intense sensation of light softened and an aromatic scent drifted to him from the trees. Small insect-devouring bats flitted about and suddenly vanished in their orbit-veering flight. No word had reached him from Ann. Perhaps she had written and the letter had lost its way. Perhaps his own had failed to find her. There was no way of knowing.

There was a shriek of laughter. Turning, he saw the women clinging momentarily to each other before parting. Charlotte, the younger of the two, took a few dogged and forceful steps towards her hut and fell like a stone. Another burst of gormless laughter issued from Sally who swayed uncertainly with a heavy milking pail in her hand. Her suetty face held an unnatural carmine flush. One of the workmen went to the aid of Charlotte only to be greeted with a string of violent obscenities. She regained her feet, grimaced, and with sluggish movements made her own way to her door. Drunk. Joseph wondered how they had come by the rum. He pursed his lips. He felt sorry for Charlotte. She was young but had succumbed to a terrible acquiescence in this place. Theft in faraway Leicestershire had cast the die of destiny for her. Her young life wasted for want of opportunity.

'Holy Mother of God I'll give it to you!' Sally shouted in a high sharp voice as she attempted to put a young milking cow into the bails. She too was sometimes on her feet and sometimes not. Succeeding at last, she tugged the leg rope violently, swore as she sat down, and began pulling at the cow in a lumpen mass of anger and resentment.

A stranger sat at the wooden table drinking rum with Bert, the free man, from chipped enamel mugs. The woman, May, stood near the rusted chimney space tending to a pot of boiling mutton.

'This is Stan Larkin,' said Bert. 'He's takin' some cattle through to Parramatta from up on the Murrumbidgee.'

The man did not get to his feet. He looked at Mason but not exactly into his eyes allowing himself a thin smile. He was young, square-shouldered, his face was strong, lean, but narrow, emphasising his uneasy, calculating eyes.

'Ya timed it well,' said the woman to Mason as she heaped a metal plate for him at the table. Her faded red hair was pulled back into an untidy bun. It was not hard to read in her eyes what she had lived through. She too poured herself some rum when she sat down. While Macarthur, unlike many of his equals, paid his assigned convicts ten pounds a year in cash, he did allow the retail of spirits to free workers on his farms in exchange for labour. Mason knew that Bert and May were in debt after doing work worth as much as forty or fifty pounds because of their addiction to the spirit.

Bert wore a sleeveless sweated under vest. His greying hair mussed over his forehead. He lightly scratched his bare forearm tattooed with a swallow. He was once a sailor and half believed that the bird had helped him to return to dry land.

'Blacks eh!' he exclaimed.

Mason's appearance had obviously interrupted the flow of Stan's conversation.

'Bargaining don't work. The gun is the only way.'

'You must be joking,' said Mason impetuously, 'you don't shoot them, do you?'

'Ya rather have a spear in ya guts, would ya?' His voice was without inflection. His eyes had become steely and intense. He gave a jeering laugh, 'You'd shoot a native dog running amok in the flock, wouldn't ya? The settlers are stretchin' further and further out up there way beyond the boundary of the colony. The blacks won't leave the sheep alone. We've killed seven of the buggers on the place. I tell ya it's war.'

Unsettled, Mason determined not to say another word. He could see the glint of sharp pleasure in the man's eyes, like lust, and again, the tight excited smile. He could have been talking about a hunting trip.

'One fella we called Major. You wouldn't believe it, May. He could speak a little English as good as ya please. "What for you white fellows come and sit down on our land?" he would shout. He was a real cheeky bugger.' Stan sneered silently and took a swig of rum. 'Found him by himself one day and shot him, point blank. I rolled him down a bank and into the river. But I was worried, I can tell ya. All night I worried that his mob would find him there and come lookin' for me. So next mornin' I get up and go back to the place. There he was plain as day stuck in a tangle of branches from a tree that had fallen into the river. His head was clear above the water. The eyes were gone. Birds had been at him, I guess. I was shakin' I can tell ya! Me life wouldn't have been worth a sixpence if his mob showed up then. I waded out into the water. It was damn cold too and poked him free with a stick so he would float away.'

He paused. His face stilled with secrets.

'This is a nice lump of meat, May. Ta.'

Mason lay in the darkness of his tiny room listening to the night sounds. Tired as he was, he could not sleep. The window was open. His back uncovered to the sullen breeze. Beyond the window the darkness was limitless. He remembered being taken through the forest one night soon after arriving at Westwood to see the blacks perform a dance. Young men only engaged in it, the older ones contented themselves with looking on. The women sat on the ground around an earthen circle cleared of branches and stones. Their possum skin cloaks were rolled up into a ball on their laps and these they beat with their hands in time with the sharp clack of the sticks the dancers carried. The youths were naked except for a thin belt around the waist from which was suspended a small mat of possum fur at the front only. They had decorated themselves with white pipe clay which contrasted strikingly with their black skin and gave them a wild, savage appearance. They jumped violently on powerful legs accompanied by loud grunts, making something like the sound of a workman using a heavy rammer or crowbar. Finally, they had all squatted down and putting their hands under their thighs jumped wonderfully, perhaps in imitation of a kangaroo. Their bodies rippled with strength and glistened with rubbed fat and sweat. Raising their voices to the highest pitch, all had ended in a great whoop as they twirled and separated. It was as if the cry came from the earth itself, ancient and in some way deeply significant, but it was as remote from him as the hidden stars above the trees. Those trees where they had danced were gone. Macarthur's cattle now grazed on their dancing ground.

He rolled over. Fidgeted. Thought of the next day's labour.

No, it was no use. He got up, pulled on his shirt and left the kitchen. The moon was a glow of diffused brightness behind a thin smear of clouds. A dog stirred, barked once before recognising him, and settled back into the shadows. How far away Ann was! And Eliza! Time means little to a small child, but he wondered if she would know him now? Would she run without hesitation into his arms to greet him?

A shadow moved. Stan Larkin was leaning casually against the door jamb of the workers' hut. They caught each other's eye, a mutual contempt was registered. Joseph nodded unsmiling. Stan ignored him with sombre mockery and with an air of languid boredom sauntered out into the silvery half-night towards Charlotte's hut. The door opened. His face was splashed with candlelight. There were muffled sounds, and then a long drawn out, 'Sta-an!' The man laughed.

Joseph winced in momentary confusion before turning his back on them. Yes, there was more to the story of that exposed corpse pilloried in air amongst broken wood than Stan would tell. The fault would rest more with the likes of Larkin than the blacks. And who could blame them for their spirit and futile revenge against such men? Mason would often come back to that last glimpse of Stan slouching in the doorway, his eyes full of scorn and malice. It had revealed his own capacity for hatred.

Bullington, Hampshire
14th July 1832

My dearest husband,

I have little skill with the pen as you know, but I want to write this to you myself. It is an odd feeling that this letter will travel so far and take so long before you read it. Much may happen in our lives in that time.

We were overjoyed to recieve your letter and to no that you are not mistreeted or in any great dainger. I could almost here your voice and imagine how you looked. Your mother is in good health and Eliza is now a little girl. We want for nothing. People, especially the Deacles, have been very good to us. If only you were here!

Your mother has written to Robert. He will no by now, poor man, that Margaret Thomas who he was so fond of is married. The man is a servent to Sir Thomas Barrents and she hopes to be a kitchen maid up at the big house. Poor Robert!

Joseph, I miss you. I love you. Keep yourself safe for our sake. We must have hope that one day somehow we will be together again.

Yours
Ann

25

JOSEPH LIFTED HIS eyes to the screeches and screams of the cockatoos above him in the branches of a stunted gum. The large raucous birds, white as salt, strutted along the broken limbs of the tree, their eyes bead-bright. Two or three lifted their vivid yellow crests in agitation or alarm before the whole flock swooped off in a hurried swirl of frantic shrieks. The summer that had lasted so long had died into days of cool mornings and midday warmth. Below him in the steep stony gullies the rough barked trees looked soft in the mist. Their grey-green leaves smoky in the diffused light. Distant valleys were filled with fog. Craggy hills loomed above the broad sheet of white light and beyond them were the mountains. He knew he had miles to walk that day if he were to see his old shipmate Levi, but he paused in awe at the scene around him. He liked the noises of early morning. The skirl of unseen plovers in wet grass. The clear warble of butcher birds. The flapping and quarrelling snowstorm of cockatoos which had settled in a tree a quarter of a mile away. For the first five miles or so there had been some sort of track but since he had crossed the Western Road which went over the Blue Mountains to the west, he had seen no one nor any sign of human habitation. He hoped he was keeping to a reasonably straight line through the bush.

In his pocket he carried Ann's letter. It never left him. It had buoyed his spirits for weeks. Why had it taken so long to reach him? Where had it been? But all was chance. How well he understood that now! He had seen bags of mail exchanged at sea in the hope that the passing ship would arrive safely at its destination. It was chance that Ross Lane had not been killed when his dray loaded with lime had overturned on his way up from Parramatta. His bullocks had tired on a steep hill and had moved backwards crashing the dray through a wooden fence. Luckily the jerk had shaken the iron pin out that held the bullocks to the pole of the dray which saved them but not the dray which had careered down an embankment. Lane had crawled out unhurt from under the lime with Ann's letter still intact. It was chance too that he had learned from Lane that Levi Brown who had sailed with him on the *Eleanor* lived at Vermont, not twenty miles north of Westwood.

He came to a newly made wooden fence, slipped through the rails and went down to a creek that outlined the rise on which the house and farm buildings stood. The men's slab huts were hovels, some covered with shingles, others with bark. Someone was chopping wood. Each blow rang out pistol-sharp. Blue films of smoke drifted from makeshift chimneys. A stooped man straightened, grinned and brandished his spade in welcome. Levi! Dogs flung themselves at the end of their chains barking wildly until a curt voice reduced them to a whimpering discontent. Levi's clothes were little more than rags. He wore no boots. His face was lean and careworn from work and weather but smiling as he embraced Mason in an iron grip.

'There has always been talk of pardons. It's easy to talk. Even easier to dream. But nothin' will come of it,' Levi said shifting in the grey half-dark of the men's quarters. 'This is home now. Forget the old country. We will never see it again.'

The place smelled of damp and unhappiness. Mason was sure there were fleas. He had hoped to spend the night but now realised he would not. Levi could offer no butter, no cheese, no meat, only maize bread. 'His bloody dogs are better fed!' announced Levi in a hard voice. They drank Scotch coffee made from the scrapings of burnt bread boiled in water and drank it from a pint pannikin made of tin.

'But what of your wife and the boys?' Mason asked.

They knew every member of one another's families from endless talks and the long agony of reflection on board the *Eleanor*.

The sharpness of Levi's blue eyes dulled grew vacant and unseeing with despair.

'I'm not so young. I'm half-starved and as skinny as a weasel. Me eldest is married, perhaps he is a father himself. I dunno. I've heard nothin' at all,' he said flatly. He looked at Mason with painful vividness. 'Joe, it *was* a death sentence we got.'

Joe was silenced. He sat with his chin in his hands and looked at a shaft of dust-laden light filtering through a hole in the roof.

'We'll do our time, get a ticket of leave maybe, and then work for wages. Make the most of it here, Joe, and forget England. Stop thinkin' that life is cheating you. Take what there is and use it.' He paused, became pensive and silent for a time and then said more quietly, 'Men here often marry when they already have wives.' Self-consciousness reddened the man's face. 'The government turns a blind eye on it after seven years. That's the best the likes of us can look forward to, Joe, not bein' alone.'

He had to go. He had eighteen miles to walk to Westwood. If he reached the dusty scar of the Western Road before darkness he had little fear of becoming lost. From there the country was flat if thickly wooded and the night promised a hard sharp moon. The loneliness of the huge land already held him in its grip. Out there the world seemed uninhabited.

Levi went with him as far as the fence.

'Bye shipmate,' he said, his voice catching with emotion.

Mason nodded solemnly.

When he reached the first rise he turned. Levi was still there standing under tall spotted gums patterned with the light and shade of early evening.

Raymond Terrace
nr Newcastle, NSW
November 1833

Dear Brother,

I received your last letter with gratitude.

I too have but little news. I hear next to nothing and newspapers are a rarity here. I cannot learn if Parliament is doing anything for us, but I refuse to be cast down. I will not mourn at the grave of spent years and lost opportunities. I think of the past but thinking will not change it. And I have a will to be happy wherever I may be. I do not lack beef or bread and at times I confess I could rejoice at leaving England if I were not separated from family and long-known friends. Not one in five of the people here would ever think of returning. Their lives are not much different from what awaited them in England, but here at least they do not go hungry. With that, most seem content.

Hereabouts they say there are very fine coal pits but the government will not have them worked as they want the land cleared and you may have what wood and timber you please for the fetching. If farmer Deacle were here with his wagon and horses he would soon accumulate a fortune! We have had some good rain and our little cornfield is waist high. Beans are in fine bloom, garden peas are eight inches high and the peach orchard continues to thrive.

I am sad to hear of Levi Brown's hard lot. Sure I am that there was never a set of more harmless inoffensive men in the world than most of those who came out with us. I have often made it a subject of remark that the better the man the more severe was the sentence.

For the present I bid you adieu.

Robert

26

'How is the baby?'

'Not bad. Good considerin' the heat.'

The woman's hand moved at a fly that had settled on the child. The infant's face suddenly puckered and gave a weak petulant cry of complaint. Charlotte offered her thumb and the baby sucked noisily.

'Greedy but, like his father.' She gave a hard, faded laugh. 'I better get him out of this heat and give him a proper feed.'

But she remained standing there, the sun clinging to her dark hair. She patted the child with a patient almost abstracted air, caressing, soothing him off to sleep. He saw that the dress she wore was a very pale blue and not white as he had first thought.

Joseph gave a quick conscious smile. He was puzzled by her deliberate wounding of the self. It was familiar, yet it disturbed. The harsh set of her mouth, the passive indifference towards the opinions of others. Even with new arrivals Charlotte was unconcerned to disguise the child's history. He wasn't sure whether it was a gesture towards something she once believed in or was a kind of obstinacy, a defiance which rose in her as a defence against the world. He found himself liking her unaffected features more and more. Her undemanding face, rather round and wistful, had an old-fashioned quality to it, a certain simplicity and an unashamed prettiness. She stirred a tenderness in him. He recognised in her a counterpoint to his own loneliness – a loneliness which he felt like pain.

Stan Larkin had not returned to Westwood and Charlotte no longer drank hard spirits.

The silence felt longer than he knew it was. Her eyes which she often kept lowered suddenly met his.

'I best take him in.'

As she spoke, Joseph realised that Charlotte loved him. He had not expected this assault upon his feelings and felt a sudden rush of affection for her. He searched for words to say. It was better to end what had not really begun, but words eluded him.

He nodded. 'Yes.' Confused, he hesitated for a moment or two. He snatched futilely at words that tumbled about in his mind. He knew he should say more but could not. He turned and walked on across the sun-slashed yard.

She loved Joseph Mason. She said it silently, and said it again as he walked off.

The kitchen block smelled of onions and stifling heat. He hung back and chose instead the thin belt of shade trees. A rooster crowed, a far away sleepy sound. Someone was using a hammer. The trees drooping silver-grey leaves were motionless in the blank white glare of heat. Out of the stale sunlight he tried to compose his mind. He seemed momentarily deprived of all sensation. The thought of Ann came to him in sad reverie as if snagged by thorns in his memory. He felt her absence with a quick pathos and a rising sense of guilt. He looked out at the flat, low, uniform horizon shimmering in the heat. It was true he was fond of Charlotte. He recalled the quick pleasure of touching her fingers in taking a tea cup from her, the composed eagerness of her expressive eyes, the calm intimacy of sitting alone with her in front of her fire. He knew such moments lifted the loneliness from her, the bleakness she felt. She loved him. His narrow, quiet life seemed transformed, suddenly wrenched off course like a wind-slewed gull. An uneasy guilt twisted inside him again. He upbraided himself, but he knew with clarity that he wanted to see her again.

He started! A black man stood not three yards from him. He wore the ill-fitting remains of what were once red trousers and a small remnant of a filthy blanket drawn tight around his neck. His face textured like old brown parchment was wrinkled with anxiety or sadness. His arms and back were bare, daubed with red clay, perhaps for protection from the sun, and he carried a club that was curiously carved. The man was suffering from some terrible skin disease. Small bush flies clustered over weeping blistered eruptions on his flesh. His chest was a mess of white scabby scales.

He said something. Repeated it, but Mason could not understand him. Flies crawled across his face. His thick curly hair was clotted with grease, dried blood and dust. His mild brown eyes were watchful, filled with knowledge that Joseph could never share. He lifted his left hand palm upwards as if in supplication. He spoke again. His right hand still held the heavy club the head of which rested against the thin calf of his leg.

'What do you want?' Mason asked in a strained voice.

His words fell dead in the heat and silence. He felt a quick stab of fear.

There was noise and movement behind him. Then May was beside him in a floral dress and broken boots. She carried a sugar bag.

'There yer are ya poor bugger. Now get off with ya!'

The black man took the bag, gave a quick sideways look and set out across the tawny grass towards the distant low scrub that was deepening in colour as the beginnings of evening came.

'Leprosy. Was it leprosy?'

May laughed.

'Nah! But it may as well be. He's got the dry scall. He's gotta keep to himself till it's gone. He can't join his camp with that. He needed the pig's lard I gave him real bad. It will help the itch.'

Mason sighed in relief and looked at May as if for the first time.

SYDNEY GAZETTE, 1st OCTOBER 1835
From the English papers
WILLIAM COBBETT

*O*F WILLIAM COBBETT'S *death which we announced in* The Times *yesterday, no fact can be told that has not long been known. His origin and progress in the world – his habits and character, public as well as private, his errors, contradictions, prejudices, hatreds, unblushing effrontery – all these have for a quarter of a century been so familiar that long before his death they had ceased to inspire any lively interest.*

But take this self-taught peasant for all in all; he was perhaps in some respects a more extraordinary Englishman than any other of his time. Birth, station, employment, ignorance, temper and character in early life were all against him. But he emerged from and overcame them all. He ended by bursting that formidable barrier which separates the class of English gentlemen from all beneath them, and died a Member of Parliament, representing a large constituency which had chosen him twice.

A voluminous writer, he worked for more than forty years without, we verily believe, the interruption of so much as a single week from languor of spirit or physical weakness. For years this journal was the favourite weekly victim of his torturing sarcasm, contemptuous jocularity and fierce invective. As a political writer we pronounce him the most inconstant and faithless that ever appeared before his countrymen. His doctrines, principles and opinions lacked consistency and common honesty. They seem altogether not so much untenable as laughable. The same spirit betrayed itself after he was elected to parliament which prevented him from acquiring any weight or credit there at all proportionate to the strength and vivacity of his intellect.

So we take leave of Cobbett. He died at Barnes in Hampshire, where for the last twelve or fourteen years he greatly exerted himself in agricultural matters. Whatever his faults were, he is now at rest. He was a man whom England alone could have produced and nurtured to such self-generated power. He belonged neither to principles, to parties, nor to class. He and his writings formed a remarkable phenomenon but he has struck no root in America where his intellect first sprang to life, or in England where it ripened into almost unexplained vigour.

The Times, *Saturday 20th June 1835*

27

A MATCH DROPPED from her hand and wood-smoke coiled from the fresh pine tinder under the copper tub in the bright early afternoon. Joseph was working in a patch of garden he had made for her at the rear of the hut. Her little boy contented himself walking unsteadily in the grass about her feet and she stooped to give him some wooden clothes pegs to play with. She turned to watch Joseph. His movements were slow, heavy, deliberate. She bit her lower lip in thoughtfulness as he again reached for the grey weathered fork with his large, rough, work-hardened hands, applied the weight of his boot to it and slowly levered it back towards himself. Large, shabby thistles growing in the neglected end of the garden bent their faded purple heads against the breeze. The days were growing shorter, the afternoon shadows longer and cooler. He must have felt her gaze because he propped, smiled and waved to her.

Her arms reddened in the hot water and frothing soda of the tub. She lost herself for a while. She did not know what she thought. The warm smell of soap and clean velvety skin brought memories of her mother. Charlotte remembered herself turning pale with indignant swelling anger when she was told she was to work up at the big farm house amongst complete strangers. But she had come to like it and had considered herself fortunate. Nor did she mind the work. She recalled the heavy clank of the kettle as she put it on top of the range, the scrape of the wood box across the slate flagstones. The setting out of cups, knives and forks, all that was needed was laid out ready on the table; the toasting of bacon over the flames, the careful catching of the drops of fat on thick slices of bread. And she had loved the walk across the fields after the afternoon milking. The thin sunlight without heat. The rooks cawing, wheeling like black snowflakes across a sky of melting yellow light to settle in the branches of old beech trees beyond the corner of the lower meadow. It now seemed like a faraway dream that fatal afternoon. The house was empty, filled with the silence of aimless, afternoon lassitude. The cupboard was a jumble of materials: sewing boxes, scissors and dust – the accumulated haberdashery of years. In that still moment she took a small bolt of muslin. It was done without forethought with a quick, light movement. She had not heard the dull thuds of old Mrs Thorley's stockinged feet on the stairs.

'Why Charlotte, whatever do you have there? Alfred! Alfred, please come here for a minute.'

'I must say you look as if you are a million miles away,' Joseph said kindly.

She started. He had rammed the old garden fork into the dark resisting soil and was standing beside her, his eyes honest, searching. She closed her eyes and for some moments, rested her forehead against his chest and drew into herself the utter comfort and security of his presence.

'I'll help you with the sheets,' he said and moved towards the makeshift clothesline propped up with a dead forked eucalypt branch. The child, William, lifted his arms to him and he reached down and tickled the little boy on the ribs with both hands. The infant squirmed and twisted away from him laughing.

Charlotte smiled. She knew Joseph would have tea with her, stay until the child was settled and sleeping peacefully. She knew too, that he would then leave for his own lonely room in the kitchen with Bert and May. She would have given herself to him, given him anything, but she did not resent the steeliness of his resolve. It went beyond fierce morality, perhaps even guilt; at its core was suffering.

28

THE WOUNDS OF memory always gaped wide and bled freely at this time of year. He had endured six years of exile, almost to the day, a loneliness punctured only once in all that time with the sad joy of a single letter from Ann. Cobbett was dead. Hope was dead. A quick burst of anger seized him. Six years! Endless days each like the last, a long unbroken tissue of boredom and meaninglessness. What was England to him now? He tried to think of Ann, to remember her goodness and her fineness, to remember how she had loved him and had suffered because of him. But his thoughts and feelings about her seemed to belong to some other dimension of time; they belonged to before what had happened in a place now remote from him. What did he know of her life and circumstances now? Work helped. It could blot up feelings and wipe out thought for awhile, annul the hours – and there was Charlotte. His face expressed extreme emotion. Charlotte and her little boy were more real to him than his own family. Levi was right. He should accept that this place was his present and his future. His mind became crowded with thoughts of Charlotte. If not for her he would have become surly, a recluse, part of nothing but the farm. He would have been driven to despair long ago. Yet he had held back. Always he had held back in wordless affection. Would it cost so much to say, 'I love you'? He had become proficient at all manner of farm work whether axe or mallet, spade or rein, wool or hide. He could, he *would* make his future in this land and it would be with Charlotte. The thought lifted his spirits and drained away his melancholy.

He had tramped through the quivering heat of sun-hazed low scrub and pale-coloured grass to climb into high country, into wet forest, to follow the steep leafy gully beside a stream which tumbled in a series of narrow waterfalls. He sat on sun-warmed rocks above the falls. Here in the diffused brightness of tree-fern and green air cooled by shade and moisture, he seemed an infinite distance from anywhere. He stood and moved closer to the white noise and misting lip of the falls. The harsh majesty of the place assailed him. Below him spread the measureless expanses of a land seemingly unaltered for thousands of years. He found a beauty in its wildness and livid colours. He admired the blue of its empty distance, the vastness of its skies and the unbroken line of the horizon. It was unmappable, unknowable, a land that lived by its own laws, the growth of its trees, the free flow of its waters, and the movements of its animals. Its pulsing, living heart, and that of its people, would have to be utterly broken, for his kind to thrive within it.

He began his descent. He was filled with a desperate longing to see Charlotte, to take her in his arms and put an end to his purposeless grief. He felt almost faint with buoyant emotion. A tree had toppled. Its fall had created a circle of yellow light, an arena where new growth of glossy leaves and branches strained upwards. Flat orange fungi clustered on the crumbling trunk like embedded plates. Mason walked round the root bole. As the tree had fallen, it had torn up in its roots a circular cliff of hard earth. He stooped. Half-buried in the soil he found a flat dark stone. He worked it from the earth and brushed it clean. It fitted his palm. He would keep it. Closing his fingers around it as he moved on, it gave weight to his hand. When he left the trees, the light came like a hardening of the sky. The grass was brittle under his feet. He washed the black stone in the river. The sides and cutting edge of the stone axe had been smoothed and shaped with endless patience. How long had it been in the earth he wondered? Had it been lost? Or had a black man's hands carelessly discarded it clasping a steel tomahawk in its stead, unaware of what he was abandoning and what he was embracing in the exchange?

The day began to wear itself out. A breeze picked up. Crows wheeled in broken circles above him cawing curses on the world. A dog barked. He could see Westwood. A thin spume of smoke leaked from the rooftop of an out-building. In a rare portal moment he felt Charlotte's secret longing for his return, her anxiety succeeded by instant relief as she saw his distant, approaching figure. He increased his pace and resisted the urge to wave to her unseen across the empty space. A heavy dray was in the yard. Chickens were scratching diligently in the dust around its ponderous steel-hooped wheels. Ross Lane must be up from Parramatta. Good! He liked the man despite his silences and bluntness.

'Get to bed ya old goat before you end up in the fire,' said May curtly. Her face was a flaccid, dirty grey, almost the colour of putty.

Bert heeled over at an angle and suppressed a belch with bulging cheeks. They were both drunk on the rum that had come in the dray and they had been pecking at each other continuously for half an hour or more in sullen complaining tones. Bert reached the perpendicular, sneered silently, but obeyed, raising his hand in farewell. May followed him. There was a dull thud, a sigh. She maundered on a while longer until her slurred speech became muffled and died into silence.

Ross Lane, calm as a pond, gave Mason a sidelong look and drank the well-brewed tea poured from May's brown-stained, once white teapot.

'I have something for you,' he said, in a quiet, almost foundering voice. A shadowy smile altered his features. He had been waiting his moment. He took a folded, well thumbed letter from an inside pocket and pushed it across the table towards Mason. His hand remained on the crumpled paper. 'It was at the post office in Parramatta. It's yours by rights all said and done.' He lifted his hand free from the letter and leant back in his chair.

Across the letter was scrawled 'Refused by Mr Macarthur'. Mason recalled another letter which had come through his master's hands which had been broken open and sealed afresh. The initials on the seal had been clearly effaced and the paper slightly scorched where it had been held against a candle to melt the wax. He had said nothing but had long been suspicious that his liberty may be held from him if there were a chance of doing so. He searched the face of the older man who sat silently opposite him. Lane pursed his lips and gave him the most minimal of nods.

He broke the seal. There was a hiatus, a slowing of rushed time.

'I am a free man,' he said with a serenity that surprised him. 'I have been given a free pardon and permission to return to my native land. The money for the passage has been raised by subscription from the good people of Sutton Scotney.' Excitement was now palpable in his voice; a sudden euphoria had seized him. He could have taken Lane in his arms and danced with him around the cramped room shouting wildly into the night. 'I am a free man!'

'Not quite,' said Lane in a laconic drawl, stirring his tea unnecessarily, 'at least, not yet. You must wait until your name appears in the *Sydney Gazette*. Until it appears there you cannot leave Macarthur or take any steps towards returning to England.'

'But, but…' gurgled Mason in a harsh whisper edged with an urgent stridency.

Lane relented. His face wore a benevolent, clever expression. Again he reached into the folds of his coat and placed on the table a recent copy of the *Gazette* and beside it another letter. His eyes began to smile. 'I have been keeping a close eye out for you.' He tapped the newspaper meaningfully. 'You, Joseph Mason are at this moment a free man. You are not beholden to Macarthur or any other living man.'

They stood and Lane clasped Mason firmly by the hand then held his shoulders in an awkward half-embrace. Joseph felt his eyes suddenly water and glanced away. It was then that he saw that the unopened letter still lying on the scrubbed and pitted surface of the table was from Ann.

He broke the dry, cracked seal. It was dated 1834. Ann had written it three years ago!

My dearest husband,

I hope beyond hope that you recieve this letter. We are all well but we live in deep fear that some misfortune has befallen you as we have heard nothing from you. I no in my heart that you must write to me but the mail is so uncertain. You are so far from us!

I pray that you will recieve this as I write to give you hope. Sutton Scotney has witnessed a great event. William Cobbett himself has visited us and held a festival to celibrate the important Bill that has passed Parlament. A tent was put up and Mr Cobbett brought a ham that weyed seventy pounds and a waggon of mutton, beef and veal and hogsheads of beer. Local farmers brought puddings, bread and cooked bacon. It was all to honour you, Joseph! You and Robert! The men who signed your petition and who are still living here had pride of place at two long tables. Enos Diddams was chairman and all were dressed in smock frocks with blue ribbons to their hats. We had to bring our own knives and forks. Mr Cobbett insisted on only one thing – no 'infurnal' potatoes were to come near the place. There was a great deal of talking and much singing.

Mr Cobbett insisted on helping to cut up the meat. He was overcome by the heat and he was taken to the inn to rest. But in the afternoon he gave a speach from the top of a waggon. He seemed very old. His hair is white and he stoops, but his voice was strong. I wish I could remember it all for you. But he spoke of you and Robert as heroes. Heroes! Your only crime, he said, was to read his newspaper and he promised to do everything in his power to bring you home to England. Hundreds of people whatched and listened to him and then cheered him. Enos is sure Mr Cobbett will be elected to the new Parlament before the end of the year. Take hope from this my husband. I am quivring like a hurt bird with excitement as I write. We pray that you may soon come home to us.

I heard from Mrs Reed that early in the morning the day after the festival, Mr Cobbett rode the three miles to Micheldever alone. There some farm workers took him to poor Henry Cook's grave. They would have found it easily enough for it is always covered in flowers. He became greatly distressed. 'Hunger!' he said. 'Hunger and want amidst plenty was the cause of this.'

Joseph, I miss you. I love you. I am your wife still, just as I was on our wedding day. You are in my thoughts. You haunt my dreams. We are waiting for you to come home.

Yours
Ann

He could not sleep. His feelings seethed in turmoil. He had not spoken to Charlotte. He had not told her the unpitying, unforgiving truth that he would leave in the early hours of the morning with Ross Lane. He walked outside in the night air, his feet bare in the cooling grass. Above the lattice work of leaves and branches, the stars were myriad bright specks which pricked into sight between moving clouds in the moonlight. The little cottage that had been built for Macarthur to spend two or three days in whenever he bothered to visit the place was edged with blocked moon-shadow. He looked at Charlotte's hut. It was lit only by her fire which threw waves of light and shadow across her window. The night was alive with soft sounds – moving eddies of leaves in the dying breeze, the hollow chirring of insects, the quick scuttle of small unseen creatures. He breathed in the darkness and the soft scent of warm bark brought out by the settling dew. He caught sight of a pale figure moving in the darkness, her white dress appearing and disappearing amongst the black trees in the moonlight.

Charlotte was running towards him. In a quick movement they drew together. They did not kiss, but held each other gently. Joseph gave a long sigh. He was filled with a heavy sense of what must be – the long journey of life without her. She looked up at him with a deep, tense, excited expectation. He could see she was shivering with emotion.

'You have news. Something important has happened,' she said urgently. Her dark hair strayed bleakly upon her neck.

The vehemence of her tone both touched and alarmed him.

'I am a free man. I must leave tomorrow. I must leave you, Charlotte, and go to my wife and child. I am sorry.' He said it softly. The words had an intimate, protective tone. He rejected falsity for time would contradict it, perhaps ruthlessly. He knew these moments would haunt whole days.

'No! No!' She spoke it as a desolate cry. There was a momentary flash of wildness in her eyes. 'You confuse me!' Her face grew as pale as ivory. She could feel herself being sapped and broken, her life giving way to the years of solitude ahead. 'I love you, Joseph. I would go with you. To anywhere.' She looked at him pleading silently before lowering her face in defeat. She began to cry and he rocked her gently in his arms. Her face grew calmer more deliberate. 'I'll curse you, Joe Mason, but you are a good man.'

Full of remorse he could not speak. Pain transformed his face into a violent tragic mask.

'I will try very hard,' she said quietly with forlorn dignity, and began to cry again.

There was a very faint hint of light in the room, the first light of morning. Her child still slept. The silence of the morning was unbroken. That he would be gone was her first thought. He would be gone as the dead are gone. She moved to the window and the empty blue of the sky. The air was still. Ross Lane's dray was no longer in the yard. She did not weep, although she wanted to. The child stirred and called for her.

29

THE BLUE MORNING sky quickly covered over with a hot whitish film, but the bare floor of the hut still held a pleasant lingering coolness.

'I'll walk with you as far as Raymond Terrace,' Robert said, trying hard to keep his voice amiable against the threatening sadness.

Joseph met his eyes and nodded.

There had been no harsh words between them, no erosion of friendship. Silences between them were not awkward. But there had been disappointments. Joseph's first act as a free man in Sydney was to withdraw the two pounds the ship's doctor had put in the Savings Bank on their arrival in the colony and take a place in the steamer *Tamer* bound for Maitland on the Hunter River near where Robert lived at Bandon Grove. He had hoped that they would sail to England together as free men. But that was not to be. Although the newspapers and journals were teeming with extracts from the English papers declaring that all those transported for the riots of 1830 were pardoned, the *Gazette* going so far as to say they would receive a free passage home, Robert had been granted only a conditional pardon. He could not yet leave the colony. And there was Lydia.

A small woman, she had brown hair and a freckled face. She could not be more than twenty-two, Joseph thought. He studied her as she busied about the room preparing breakfast for them. 'She will be pleased when I am gone!' he thought, perhaps unfairly. The missing forefinger on her right hand seemed no disability to her, nor did Joseph find its absence grotesque.

It was her dove-grey eyes which disturbed him. There was a hardness in them, a look of cautious watchfulness, something slightly predatory as if her security lay in a constant mistrust. She would not be drawn about her past. Joseph knew nothing about her beyond the fact that she had been transported to New South Wales and now lived openly with Robert as his wife. Yes, her eyes disturbed him, and her tattoos. Those mulberry-stained letters permanently inked on her upper arm: PC SM LM. Were those crudely shaped letters the clue to her past life in England? LM – Lydia Mills. Who then was PC? SM? But Robert would brook no criticism of her. 'Nothing could prevent us coming together,' he had said emphatically when Joseph had privately pleaded caution about his domestic arrangements.

New South Wales had changed Robert. A genuine thoughtfulness had replaced his more familiar youthful and buoyant moods that Joseph remembered from yesteryear. He had always been a noisy critic of the self-enriching ruling class with their titles inherited, purchased or corruptly obtained who ground the poor into dust, but something else had entered his soul with a jagged edge to it leaving him with a distaste for anything respectable or refined. He was at home with the workers on the farm in a way Joseph could never be. Oblivious to their starkly obscene speech and coarse humour, he had all the ease of a jovial publican in a country beer house when in their company. A distance had opened up between them. Robert had yielded himself to this hard land, accommodated himself to its differences, its absences. Joseph had not.

The dog that had seemed so determined to accompany them fell back and finally abandoned them for the dusty shade of the yard. Insects swarmed about them in the thick heat, stinging their hands annoyingly. Paper-bark trees that stretched out into tannin-brown pools shrilled incessantly with cicadas. Robert stopped. An egret, salt-white against the dark water, lifted lazily away from them. He stood watching it until it was gone behind the screen of trees out beyond the reed beds.

'They're common enough,' said Robert. 'Beautiful, but,' he added in admiration pulling back his strong shoulders.

Joseph wondered at his brother's sense of knowing the place. For him the land despite its beauty remained alien. He had never felt completely at ease with it.

The air was hot, weary. Muted distant thunder rumbled in the silver haze as they neared the roiled, muddy river where they must part.

Joseph posed the question tentatively, 'Perhaps a church wedding, Robert, before you come home?'

Robert scoffed at his brother's awkward subtlety. He was beyond any pallid lesson of caution Joseph had to offer him.

'I am resolved never again to disgrace myself by going into a church. It is the resort of the hypocrite and the profane. If my life has taught me anything it has taught me that.'

The steamer rounded the bend upstream and came into full sight.

'Joseph,' said Robert more gently, 'let us part as friends as well as brothers. We will meet again, all being well, on the soil that gave us birth before another year is out.'

A whistle from the *Tamer* lanced the silence. They shook hands firmly and Joseph stepped into the smaller boat that would take him to the waiting steamer. Robert was quickly out of sight and Joseph lowered his raised hand.

30

J OE MASON TURNED his gaze from the achingly bright sun
dazzle on the water and leaning against the bulwarks scanned
the slopes of the harbour strewn with straggling eucalypts and
rocks reflecting glassy glints of sea light. It was a bright wind-
buffeted morning. The warm cloudless sky was brilliantly blue.
The ship lifted and hissed ploughing an evanescent furrow
through the silvered skin of the water. White gulls wheeled and
twisted over the white water of the wake. He was largely oblivious
to the cheery shouts, the orders delivered tersely from the poop
deck, the moil of lean-faced sailors busy with sheets and sail as
they laughed and talked. He drew in deep drafts of sea-fragrant
air, tasted the tang of salt on his lips. He had left his brother in
early January anxious, almost desperate, to depart the colony.
He had been told by Mr Walker, a merchant and shipping agent
in Sydney, of a ship that would sail on the first day of February
and to this he agreed. He had little money and was a complete
stranger to the town but had managed to find cheap lodgings
and work on the docks helping to winch enormous bales of
wool aboard various vessels. On the 29th of January he received
a letter from Mr Walker saying that the ship would now sail on
the 26th. Somehow or other the letter had been delayed. Almost
overwhelmed with frustration, he made new arrangements with
Walker to sail on the *William Bryan* that would sail on the 12th
of March. The evening before she was to sail her cargo of wool
was fully loaded, the decks well scrubbed and the seams sealed
with pungent pitch. The ship's carpenter was fastening down
the hatches when a thunderstorm swept in from the south-west.

Lightning brought the top gallant mast of the ship crashing to the deck shivering the yards to splinters and splitting the mast to its heel. It was now late April and the *William Bryan* was almost clear of the Heads of Sydney Harbour.

He was filled with an irrational dread of seeing the last of the land. It would be the final parting. He thought of Charlotte and his heart ached for her. He would have gladly suffered much physical pain rather than this searing sadness. He would be forever riven, torn between two different hemispheres where there had been love – and pain. The past was all empty melancholy, the future all uncertainty. But the future pulled at him powerfully. The ship shuddered and began to roll and plunge through long swells of fathomless ocean. The great cerulean sky rose up from the darkening heave of sea. He looked out through salt tears at empty watery miles radiating out in all directions.

31

H E SEARCHED THE passing faces of the town – some were thoughtful, some nursed pain or disappointment, some were alight with humour – but they were strong faces, Hampshire faces. He recognised no one. He himself could pass for a sailor. A salt and sun-worn face, skin tanned a deep walnut shade. He left the noise and movement of the cobbled streets behind him, and set out across a long-grassed wet field. It was an afternoon of weak sunshine and light showers – the sort of rain that lifts one's spirits rather than depresses them. A mist was lying on the ground and it stretched upwards to an ocean of coppery clouds where fragments of broken rainbows made brief appearances. He stopped. There, propped in the grass, long-legged and long-eared sat a hare, still and alert as a sentry. It was close enough to see moisture clinging to its fur and whiskers, its shy inquisitive face. Then it was off making its long curved run. Joseph watched it, smiled sadly and walked on steadily for a mile or so where he reached a narrow road.

Mauve and pink stock, pale blue delphiniums, blur-bronze cat-mint, grew in the little gardens of the occasional stone houses. Rain again. He lifted his face to the cleansing grip of cold. It was autumn. Already an apple or two had dropped. He halted again. To his left was a large stone barn sharp-edged against the sombre grey hues of the sky. In a week or two it would resound with the rhythmic slap of leather flails and the dry showers of grain spilling on wood. The air would be astringent with the smell of men at work. Dust and tiny bits of chaff and husk would float in the glaucous light. The sun was sinking behind sun-tinged clouds. The colours multiplied – lemon yellow, ink blue. He must hurry.

He was close now. He walked in a trance of memory. Bullington! The squat, weathered brick tower of the church rose up out of the shades of darkness all around. And then, suddenly, there was his cottage. His gardens were grass. Wind rasped dead leaves across the path. Overgrown laurels obscured an entire wall. It had a fugitive look about it. They would not stay here. He was a marked man. Who would employ him? The pious Barrents still held sway in the valley. He would work hard, perhaps he could get a small holding somewhere he was not known. Sell enough produce and livestock to pay his rent and taxes. He could hope for no more than a hand to mouth existence. The fluttering light of a candle moved in the cottage. His heart lurched with a multitude of powerful emotions. He clenched his fists to quieten the trembling of his fingers and walked towards his home.

Ann started at a half-heard sound. She glanced at the old lady but it seemed she had heard nothing. She sat silently in her chair and would soon go to her bed. Eliza slept beside a handful of new flames in the rusty grate. Ann lifted a smoky, unpleasant tallow candle, moved to a little window and looked out at the lonely colours of the night. In the candle glow it could be seen that time had put a mask on her face, webs and traceries, but gently incised. Before her lay half a lifetime. It came again. A soft but unmistakable knock at the door. She met the dark eyes of Joseph's mother. A flick of fear moved in them. For a confused instant, Ann thought it was Henry Cook.

'Ann. Ann, it's Joseph.'

The old lady uttered a strange unintelligible sound and made as if to rise. But Ann was already at the open door, the candle she had held lay dashed on the flagstones. For a moment she stood before him. Her chest heaved. She could not speak.

'Ann, I have come home!'

He put his arms around her and closed his eyes tightly for a moment or two. She buried her face into his chest and wept.

AUTHOR'S NOTE

After Robert and Joseph Mason made their farewells to each other at Raymond Terrace they never met again. Joseph eventually established himself at Moors Farm, a small holding at Winnersh near Wokingham where he died on the 3rd of October 1863. No doubt he took a lively interest in the Chartist Movement between 1837 and 1854 which attempted to build an independent political party representing the interests of the labouring and underprivileged sections of the nation, but there is no evidence to suggest he ever took an active political role in Berkshire.

Robert Mason married Lydia Clarke (née Mills) and became a publican in Dungog, New South Wales. Lydia died in 1858. She was forty-eight years old. Robert Mason visited England, but not until 1864. English people and their manners seemed alien to him and he felt ill at ease and a stranger in the country. He sailed for Nelson, New Zealand, where he lived with his adopted daughter and her family. He died there on the 22nd of March 1866 at the age of eighty-one.

Joseph Carter, who stoically refused to give evidence against the Masons and so perhaps saved them from hanging with Henry Cook, was not transported but served two years on the hulks in Portsmouth.

Henry Cook was buried in the churchyard at Micheldever. Its exact location is unknown. A story persisted into the twentieth century that the snow never fell on his grave.

Joseph Mason's friend and fellow convict on the *Eleanor*, Levi Brown, remained in New South Wales. He was given permission by the government on the 21st of July 1846 to marry Elizabeth Skinner. He died in 1852 aged sixty years.

A Servant of the Governor is an historical novel based on actual events surrounding the Swing Riots in England in 1830 and their aftermath. It is a work of fiction but where possible people's real names have been used. The story of the struggle and suffering of the Dever Valley radicals is little known even in Hampshire. *A Servant of the Governor* is an attempt to historically rescue those village workers as worthy political agents who challenged injustice in defence of their rights. They should not be forgotten.

My primary sources in depicting the historical backgrounds in *A Servant of the Governor* have been *The Convicts of the Eleanor: Protest in Rural England New Lives in Australia* by David Kent and Norma Townsend (Merlin Press, London, 2002) and Joseph Mason's own vivid account of his time in Australia, *Joseph Mason: Assigned Convict 1831–1837* edited by David Kent and Norma Townsend (Melbourne University Press, Melbourne, 1996).

I am indebted to the Hampshire Record Office in Winchester for their assistance in providing typescripts of letters written by Joseph and Robert Mason.

I sincerely thank my editor Eifion Jenkins for his careful reading and astute suggestions.

Finally, I offer my heartfelt thanks to my wife Margaret for her unfailing support and encouragement.

Also by the author:

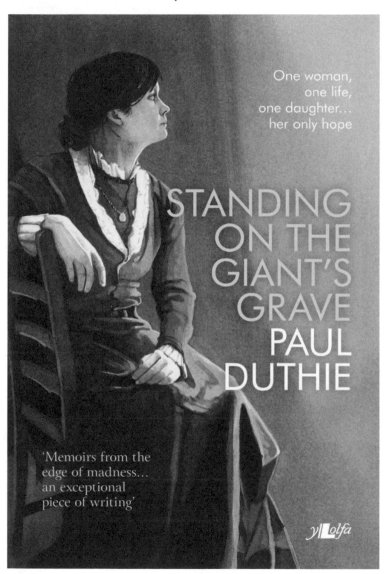

One woman,
one life,
one daughter...
her only hope

STANDING
ON THE
GIANT'S
GRAVE
PAUL
DUTHIE

'Memoirs from the
edge of madness...
an exceptional
piece of writing'

yLolfa

£8.95